The Isle of Demons

Charles O. Goulet

Writers Club Press
San Jose New York Lincoln Shanghai

The Isle of Demons

Published by Writers Club Press
an imprint of iUniverse.com, Inc.

For information address:
iUniverse.com, Inc.
620 North 48th Street
Suite 201
Lincoln, NE 68504-3467
www.iuniverse.com

ISBN: 0-595-09650-6

Printed in the United States of America

1. The Request

The dark-haired girl shook her head sending her thick tresses flying. Her green eyes sparkled merrily. Her voice tinkled. "Uncle, I'm so happy to see you again."

The tall, robust man in the azure velour cape and the tall, black felt hat opened his arms wide in invitation.

The girl flung herself into his arms, her arms entwining around his neck. He folded her in his embrace and kissed the top of her head. "My dear, how I've missed your sweet, smiling face. I'm sorry that I couldn't be here in your sorrow, but I was thinking of you as your father was laid to rest."

She stepped back and looked up into his face. "I know you would have been here if you could." Her voice was sober. She surveyed the man before her; at forty-one years old, her uncle, Jean-Francois de la Rocque, Sieur de Roberval, was a handsome man. He looked like the courtier that he was. His dark brown hair, neatly trimmed, curled in soft waves to the layered collar that enclosed his throat in a wide, white band. His grey eyes flashed in his deeply tanned face while his narrow mustache wriggled in unison with his animated mouth.

"Uncle, you look as if you've just come from the court."

His eyes twinkled. "I have. I came as soon as I heard that your father had died. He and I had important business to discuss."

She cocked her head. "What was that?" Her green eyes peered at him, searching his face.

"It's in the will, my dear. Your father was always interested in my activities. He invested in the settlement that I plan to establish in the New World in Canada."

"Oh, yes, I heard him talk about it many times. That's the land that Jacques Cartier discovered, isn't it?"

"Yes, it is, my dear. At this moment he's there with five ships and about 400 settlers. I'll join him as soon as possible. It's too late this fall, so I'll be leaving in the spring…with three ships and 200 more settlers."

"Oh, Uncle, that sounds exciting."

"Oh, it is. I hope this will lead to the Orient…to spices…or to gold, like the Spanish in their colonies…to other riches…and, of course, it's a great opportunity for glory…a chance to convert the inhabitants of the land to the true God. My salvation will be assured."

She moved toward a small, ornate table where two upholstered chairs stood on either side of it. She waved her hands toward them. "Uncle, you must join me for a glass of claret and some sweetmeats."

He waited till she sat down, then he joined her. She took a tiny, silver bell from a small tray and tinkled it daintily. Its chime drifted through the room.

A white-haired servant in dark livery glided into the room, approached her, and bowed at the waist slightly. "You rang, Mademoiselle Marguerite?"

"Please bring us some claret and some sweets."

The servant left quietly as she turned back to her uncle. "That will be the first French settlement in the New World?"

"It will, my dear. And I'm happy that our gracious King Francis has made me his viceroy and lieutenant general. It's a great honor."

"Uncle, you've served him well in the wars. It's only right that he should reward you so. Where is this land of which you speak?"

His eyes grew animated. He smiled. "It's far to the west, beyond the great fishing banks that our fishermen go to each year. It's beyond the land where they dry their fish and replenish their water supply. It's in the land of the strange people that Cartier brought to the king's court on his second voyage…the one he ended in 1535. I'm sure your father spoke of these strange men that Cartier brought to court."

"Oh...the Redskins, I think he called them."

Roberval laughed. "Yes, but they don't have red skin. It's more brown than red. They're Indians."

"Will they let you settle in their country?"

"I'm sure they will. They're friendly with our fishermen. They want to trade everything they have for our metal tools. It seems that they don't have much metal...or metal tools. But they don't have much to trade."

"What do you mean, Uncle?"

"The only thing they trade with us is furs—beaver skins, sealskins, wolf...and others."

"What can we do with those furs?"

"Our people use them for clothes. Our hatters find the beaver fur the best kind for making felt hats. But I'm sure there's gold in their lands...and other precious metals."

"Why do you want to start a French settlement there?"

"Look at what the Spanish have done in the south. They've found gold...and silver...and sugar. Our country needs settlements like that if we are to get wealth from that land. And we'll start a new society...one that's perfect."

She laughed, and her laughter rippled through the room. "Uncle, how will you do that?"

He looked at her carefully, studying her smiling face. But he did not smile. "My dear, if people live in a perfect society, they'll become perfect. We'll live in harmony with each other, as Our Lord wanted us to. I'll be the commander of the colony; there'll be an enlightened aristocracy and the rest of the people will be treated fairly and honestly."

"Where will all these perfect people come from?"

He paused, then answered slowly. "Many of my friends at court have joined me. Many have come from the farms. Many..."

"Uncle, I've heard that most have come from the prisons."

"Yes, that's true, Marguerite, but I've chosen them with care. Most are poor debtors. Their only crime is that they cannot pay their debts. So

I've given them a new chance. Some are even nobles who have lost their lands and money."

That was true, because she knew of a young man of her acquaintance from Amiens who was one of those unfortunates. She remembered his handsome face. His dark eyes flashed before her, and she recalled when they met. That was a year ago when he and his family attended a party at the neighboring castle. His wit and smile had captivated her. He'd been interested in her too, but a few weeks later she learned that he'd been thrown in jail because he could not pay his debts. Last week she heard that he would be going with her uncle to the new land.

"Uncle, do you think you could take me with you? There's nothing for me here. Now that father's gone, I'm alone. You're my nearest relative, and I do have an interest in your project." She looked at him through her eyelashes. "Some of my money is invested in it."

His eyebrows raised. The idea had never entered his head.

2. The Answer

Marguerite poured the amber wine from the silver decanter into the tiny silver cups. She set it down, and raised the small platter with its fancy pastries to her uncle. He took a delicate golden cookie covered with gleaming honey. He nodded to her.

"Uncle, do you think you could take me with you?"

He lifted the shiny wine cup to his lips as he studied his niece. Was she serious? Did she want to come with him, or was she teasing him? Did he want her along? She was a sturdy girl, just past her eighteenth birthday. True, she was now alone. Her mother had died three years before of the ague, and now her father had died of some unknown malady, suddenly. But did he want her with him? She'd be an added responsibility.

She set her tiny cup on the table. Why was her uncle hesitating? Didn't he want her with him? After all, he was attempting a perfect society. She liked that. She could fit into a perfect society with ease. "Uncle, I could be one of your perfect aristocrats. I know the rules of the court. I'm a pious person. I believe in the glory of God. I think I'd be a good candidate for your court."

He smiled. If King Francis heard her, he'd probably be accused of treason. She made it sound as if he intended to be king of this settlement. "My dear, it won't be my court. It will be the king's court. I'll only preside over it."

She smiled coquetishly. "I know that, Uncle. King Francis would never be happy with that idea. He expects his nobles to pay him homage. Will you take me with you?"

"Why do you want to go to Canada? It's a long journey...by ship...crowded...uncomfortable. Have you ever been on a long sea voyage, my dear?"

"No."

"A ship at sea is not a comfortable conveyance. It'll be crowded aboard my ships...people, animals, and supplies. And most people get seasick. Have you ever been seasick? It's not a pleasant feeling. Nor is it a pleasant sight. People vomit everywhere. The smell is nauseating. And it lasts for days."

"Uncle, I don't think you want me." Her eyes twinkled mischievously. "You don't think I can make the trip."

"That's right, Marguerite. I'm not sure that you'd want to make the voyage. It will take at least a month. And it may be a difficult time...if the winds are contrary. It could take longer than that. I've heard of some ships taking almost three months to make the voyage. You'd have to share my cabin. There are only two cabins on these ships...the captain's and the commander's."

She took another sip of wine. He nibbled on the honey-coated cookie. They studied each other.

"Uncle, I'm healthy and young. I'm sure I'll be able to withstand any hardships. If others can make the trip, I'm sure I can also. And I don't mind sharing your cabin. But I must bring old Damienne with me."

Roberval grinned. Old Damienne was Marguerite's personal servant. She had been with the family so long that he didn't know how old she was. He knew she was devoted to his niece and had taken care of her since her birth. She was more a mother to the young woman than her own mother had been.

"My dear, I haven't agreed to take you with me."

"Oh, you will, Uncle. After all, I have an interest in this venture. You told me that my father had invested in it, and since I'm his sole heir, I, now, hold that interest." She spoke solemnly and soberly. She wasn't smiling.

He tipped the cup to his lips and stared at her over the rim. Maybe he should take her along. If she was serious about coming, and he didn't take her, she might cause trouble. She seemed determined and convinced that she should be part of his new society.

"Your father didn't intend to come with me to the new land. He intended to make a profit from our trade and discoveries. I can't understand why you want to come with me."

She smiled. "Uncle, you told me this was an opportunity to start a new, perfect society, based on the teaching of Christ—just, loving, and fair for all. That's why I want to go."

"But, my dear, you're young. You haven't chosen a husband yet."

"Won't there be young nobles in the colony?"

He spoke slowly. "Yes...yes, there will."

"Then maybe I can find a husband among them?" Again she saw the smiling eyes, and handsome features of Paul Le Jeune, the impoverished son of the Sieur de Montreuil. Maybe he would be aboard one of the ships. She had heard that he was going with her uncle. Her heart fluttered as she thought of him. He was handsome and dashing. He was interested in her. She found him gallant and stimulating.

"But they're poor, my dear. They're coming because they hope to make a fortune. I'm sure there are many young nobles here in France that would be happy to marry you."

"That may be true, Uncle, but would I be happy to marry them? Most of them are bores. They may be rich, but they're not very interesting."

He knew his niece had a mind of her own, but it was the first time that he had seen her determination. She was almost stubborn. The man who became her husband would have to be strong, or she would dominate him.

"And many of them are only interested in me because of my money. They know that I've inherited my father's seigniories and lands, so that's what they want. They aren't interested in me as a person. So I have no reason to stay in France."

"Marguerite, it'll be a hard life in the new colony. We'll be starting with nothing. There are no buildings...no shops...few servants...no carriages...none of the comforts that you're used to. Do you think you can stand that?"

Her voice rose, almost triumphantly. "Uncle, if you can stand life aboard ship and in your colony, so can I. You must take me with you."

"My dear, I can't take you with me. You're too young to make up your mind. Why, you're only eighteen years old. If I agreed to bring you with me, I'd feel responsible for you. I love you like my own daughter, but I think you should wait until the colony is established and well set up, then you can come with me."

She frowned. If she did not go now, she might miss her chance to get to know Paul Le Jeune. She knew he would be on one of her uncle's ships. Each time she thought of him, her desire to see him again grew stronger. Should she tell her uncle about him? No, he wouldn't agree with her choice. He'd say that the impoverished young nobleman was only interested in her money and titles. No, she couldn't tell him.

"Uncle, I must go with you when you leave. That will be a thrill. I'll help you set up your colony. I'll be there at the beginning. I'll help the priests and nuns to Christianize the natives. I'll do anything you want me to do."

"Marguerite, you must think this over carefully."

"Uncle, I have. If you don't let me go with you, I'll withdraw all my money from this project."

Roberval searched her face and eyes. She was serious. She was determined. She could cause trouble. Maybe he should let her come with him. If she was with him, he could keep her under his watchful eye. He'd know what was happening. He could control her. If he left her in France while he was in Canada, she might endanger his plan, especially if she decided to withdraw her money.

"My dear, you make it difficult for me to refuse you."

She smiled in triumph. "Thank you, Uncle. I knew you would see it my way."

3. The Departure

The harbor at La Rochelle was busy. Boats flitted between the large ships docked or anchored, their sails furled. In the distance Marguerite could see the misty outline of the islands of Re and Oleron which protected the harbor from the storms of the Bay of Biscay.

With the help of her old servant, Damienne, she dismounted from the four-wheeled carriage. The long trip from Amiens in Picardy in the northeast to La Rochelle on the west coast of France had taken two weeks. She was happy it was over.

A dark-haired sailor in a knitted shirt, ragged knee

length breeches, and heavy leather shoes approached. "Mademoiselle Marguerite de la Roberval?"

"Yes."

"I've a boat waiting for you."

Within minutes they joined the multitude of other boats that scurried about the harbor like water beetles. Her uncle waited for her at the top of the boarding ladder. "Welcome aboard, Marguerite. I hope you had an enjoyable trip." He laughed.

"Uncle, the roads of France make it impossible for any trip to be enjoyable." She reached to grasp his hand.

Once she and her servant were on the main deck, several sailors quickly brought her baggage aboard. Slowly, the three—Marguerite, her servant, Damienne, and Roberval—moved to the stern of the ship, up the narrow stairs to the quarter deck where the commander's cabin was located. Marguerite paused on the afterdeck and looked over the ship. She looked down through the opening in the deck floor to the whipstaff steering position that was enclosed by an open hutch. From her position the captain could see the sails, the decks, and the helmsman who controlled the whipstaff that moved the rudder.

"It looks very small," she mumbled half to herself.

"I told you, Marguerite, that a ship is not the most comfortable accommodation. You're lucky to have the privacy of my cabin. The rest of the passengers won't be so fortunate."

"When do we leave, Uncle?"

"I'm hoping to leave the day after tomorrow. Most of the cargo is aboard. The passengers will be the last to board. Then we'll wait for a favorable tide and wind."

"How many passengers will we have?"

"About seventy."

She gasped in surprise. The total length of the ship was no more that twenty meters. They'd be very crowded.

* * *

April 6, 1542, the weather was favorable; the sun shone through the billowing cumulus clouds that blew in from the south and as the tide ebbed, the three ships left the harbor, a large crowd of relatives and friends shouting their farewells from the timbered docks.

Marguerite stood on the high poopdeck above her uncle's cabin and watched the shouting crowd and the scurrying sailors as they climbed nimbly in the rigging setting the sails on the three masts of the warship. Marguerite could see the culverins with their long slim barrels strung out along each side of the main deck, their muzzles pointed at the closed gunports.

She turned to the tall slender woman beside her whose grey hair was pulled back from her face and tied in a large bun at the back of her head where it was held in place by a heavy net snood. She asked softly, "Damienne, have you seen Monsieur Le Jeune?"

The elderly servant nodded her head gravely. "No, Mademoiselle Marguerite, but I've heard that he's aboard. But I told you that yesterday."

Marguerite smiled, and turned her head toward the two other smaller ships that followed them out of the harbor. They were already far enough away that the shouts of the crowd were diminishing, but multitudes of gulls and terns swooped raucously about the sails of the ships as if angry that they were leaving.

"Which one is he on, Damienne?"

"I don't know, although I think he's on that bark, The Anne. But I'm not sure."

"Ah, well, we'll find out, and then we'll have my uncle transfer him to this one."

"Your uncle will never approve of that. Although he thinks highly of the young man, I'm sure he doesn't see him as a suitable husband for you."

"Damienne, you're right. What do you think?"

"I've known Robert for many years. Although his family is not wealthy, they're a good family. They're pious and God-fearing, and they've raised Robert to be the same."

Marguerite laughed. "Then why was he in jail?"

Damienne voice became sharp. "You know as well as I do. He was cheated. That's why he owed so much money."

"I know that, but Uncle doesn't think that's a good reason for being in jail. Nobles should never be poor."

At that moment her uncle mounted the steep stairs that led to the poopdeck. He was dressed as a military officer: a large brimmed, high crowned black felt hat with a dancing white ostrich plume shaded his tanned face. A satin tunic of blue and white vertical stripes with flowing white sleeves came above his knees. A leather belt encircled his waist and from it dangled a long sword in a metal scabbard. His breeches billowed beneath his tunic to below his knees where they were drawn snugly around his legs by a narrow blue ribbon. Blue silk stockings covered the lower part of his legs, and on his feet he wore low square-toed shoes with large bronze buckles at the insteps.

It was the clank of his sword against the narrow stairs that alerted Marguerite to his arrival. He came up beside her at the stern rail of the poopdeck.

"My dear, this is perfect sailing weather, but don't think that every day will be as comfortable as this one."

"I know, Uncle." Her voice sounded resigned with a touch of annoyance. "All the passengers are safely aboard?"

"Yes, we are seventy-seven on this ship. There are seventy on "The Anne." He pointed to the nearest ship, which was now at full sail, its square sails billowing in the freshening breeze. Then he swung his arm to the other, a squat-hulled barque, which seemed to wallow as it ploughed through the white-capped waves. "And sixty

three on the 'Lechefraye'."

"Who are the captains?"

"Monsieur La Brosse captains "The Anne" while Monsieur Frotte is on the "Lechefraye." You've already met the captain here, Monsieur Sauveterre."

"Is Monsieur Le Jeune on one of your ships?"

He looked at her sharply.

"You know, Uncle, he's from back home…near Amiens."

"Yes, I know. I rescued him from prison. The young idiot lost all his money gambling and ended up in a debtor's jail. If I hadn't convinced him he should come with me, he'd still be languishing in that filthy prison. Do you know him?"

"I've met him once or twice. He seems to be a well-mannered young man."

"That he is, but he's penniless."

"Would you transfer him to this ship. It would be enjoyable to have someone from Picardy to talk to."

Her uncle shrugged his shoulders. "You've nothing in common with him, my dear. His family opposes the king. They've lost most of their lands. They're poor with little chance of recouping their losses in the future…unless this young scalawag shows he's worth anything in the New World."

"But, Uncle, the trip'll be long, and tiring, and boring. It would be nice to have someone my age to associate with."

"Out of the question. I need that young man where he is. He has his duties aboard that ship. I'll hear no more of that." His voice was sharp and determined.

"But…"

"No more." He turned away and hurried down the steep stairs to the quarterdeck below where he joined the captain.

Marguerite fumed. She turned to Damienne. "Why, he ignored me completely. He wouldn't listen."

Old Damienne nodded her head gravely, but said nothing.

The next three days Marguerite spent confined to her bed as she suffered a mild case of seasickness. She wasn't well enough to leave the cabin or her bed or to take any food. The very thought of food made her retch and feel more nauseated, so she kept her mind on other things. The handsome face of Robert Le Jeune was pleasant medicine. So she tried to devise a plan that would put the young man aboard her ship. Everything she thought of seemed foolish and unlikely to achieve her purpose.

Toward the evening of the third day, she rose from her bed and called Old Damienne to her side. Fortunately her servant had not suffered from the rolling and dipping of the ship. "Damienne, I've been thinking of a way to get Robert aboard this ship, but I can't think of any. You're old and wise. Maybe you could help me."

The old servant looked at her ward. "My dear, you'll be able to see the young man when we get to the New World."

"But, Damienne, I want him to know that I'm here…that I exist. I want him to know that I care."

The servant's wizened face broke into a grin. "My dear, there'll be plenty of time to become acquainted when we arrive in the new land."

Marguerite's brow wrinkled in annoyance. "But I'm bored now."

4. Landfall

Fog swirled about the limp sails and wet decks of the small ship as tiny waves lapped against its heavy planked hull. Marguerite stared out the porthole on the starboard side of the spare, cramped cabin. Each day on the long trip the cabin seemed to get more confining, especially when the weather was bad, and she and her old servant were limited to it.

Visibility was reduced to a few hundred yards so she could not see the two other ships that made up their convoy. They had left La Rochelle along France's western shore on April 6 and today was Thursday, June 8, over two months later. Marguerite was tired of the ship: its rolling motion, its tedious routine, its monotonous diet, its confining area, and particularly her domineering uncle.

He seemed to think that she had to obey his every command, no matter how unreasonable it was. She resented his insistence at keeping her isolated from most of the people aboard the ship, especially the soldiers that were aboard.

She turned from the porthole to Damienne. "When did Uncle say we'd arrive?"

Damienne raised her head from where she was packing clothing into a large leather trunk. "If the fog lifts, we'll enter the harbor later today. But he also said that the fogs around here can last for days and we'll have to wait until visibility is good enough to go through the Narrows."

Marguerite twisted her lips in annoyance. "What are the Narrows?"

"They're the entrance to the harbor. To enter we must pass through a very narrow channel with steep rock cliffs on either side. Once through that channel we enter a natural well-protected bay. That's why the fishermen from many countries come to this place—St. John's."

"Damienne, how do you know that?"

"I heard your uncle and the captain talking. They pay no attention to an old servant like me. You'd be surprised at the things I hear." She laughed raucously, ending in a high-pitched giggle.

Marguerite turned back to the porthole. To her right, the fog glowed and the grey veil lifted magically. Through the mist she could make out the ghostly outline of a ship, its sails hanging limply ready to catch any breeze. "The fog's lifting," she squealed joyfully. "We may land today."

A cooling breeze wafted through the open porthole. A sail snapped sharply above her. She heard a strident yell from the main deck. Then another from the quarter-deck. "The fog's lifting. There's a breeze. Prepare to make way."

Marguerite twisted to look at the working Damienne. "We should be anchored by evening, and we can set foot on solid earth again."

Damienne nodded her head.

Within minutes the fog dissipated, the sun shone clearly from a bright blue sky, a breeze from the south-east filled the sails, and the ship moved gently forward over a rippling sea—perfect for entry into St. John's harbor.

Marguerite left the small cabin and climbed the steep steps to the poopdeck to join her uncle who was surveying the ships as they closed in on the narrow entrance to the harbor. She muttered as she watched the ship maneuver to enter the narrow channel, "If the winds are wrong that would be a difficult harbor to enter."

Her uncle leaned on the long silver headed cane that he carried. "We're fortunate to have such a capable captain as Monsieur Sauveterre. It's a tricky entrance, but I'm told that the harbor is one of the best."

To Marguerite, the ship seemed to be heading straight for the high rock cliffs that loomed before them. A shout from the captain relayed to the mate and then to the helmsman soon had sailors tugging on lines as the ship veered to the right. Then Marguerite saw the opening to the harbor and understood why it was called the Narrows. Through the narrow opening she saw an expanse of placid water and beyond she saw the masts and hulls of several fishing ships.

"How long will we stay here, Uncle?"

He turned his head toward her. "Only long enough to replenish our water supply."

"How long will that take?"

"No more than a day or two."

"Oh, I was hoping that it would be longer than that."

"No, my dear. I'm sure Monsieur Cartier will be eagerly awaiting our arrival on the St. Lawrence. He must be wondering why we're so late. He expected us last year. We're almost a year late."

"Then he'll have much of the early work done, will he not?"

"I hope so, my dear. He's had time to build a good fort and habitations for our settlers."

Marguerite sighed. "It'll be enjoyable to live in a regular house. Firm ground will feel good again."

The sailors were experts, and within the hour the ship entered the protected bay that was St. John's harbor. Marguerite was surprised at the number of ships that lay anchored just offshore. She counted them as their ship came about and the crew dropped anchors fore and aft.

"Uncle, I didn't think this was such a busy harbor. There are seventeen ships here, carrying the colours of four nations—France, Portugal, Spain, and England."

"My dear, I'm told it's like this every year. The fishing banks just off shore are rich in cod and other fish, but particularly cod."

Marguerite looked toward the rocky shore. She could see several crude huts, but what intrigued her most was the wooden racks upon which she could see stacks of fish split and spread open.

"Why do they spread the fish upon those racks?"

"They're drying them, my dear. There are two ways to preserve the fish until they get them back to Europe—they can salt them, or they can dry them. When salt is scare, the fishermen dry them. They bring their catches to shore where they gut them and split them in two, and then they spread them on those racks and let them dry in the sun. It takes several days for them to dry properly."

"Some of those buildings look old."

"They are. Fishermen have been coming here for many years. Our fishermen have been coming here since the beginning of the century, and we've been joined by the Portuguese. As well, a few English and Spanish fishermen come each year."

"Does anyone live here throughout the year?"

"No, but sometimes a few fishermen will stay over the winter to take care of the huts and the racks. No one lives here permanently."

"Why not?"

"For one reason, Pope Alexander VI in 1494 divided the new world between Spain and Portugal by a line one hundred and twenty leagues west of the Azores drawn from Pole to Pole. For another the land is too cold in winter, or so the fishermen say."

"Then why are we going to set up a colony?"

"Because the Indians that Monsieur Cartier brought to France tell us there is great wealth in this land—gold and silver…and spices. Chief Donnacona told the king of these things…and the great Kingdom of Saguenay. This is our chance to become wealthy. And to increase the glory of France."

Already, most of the other passengers lined the rails on either side of the main deck, talking excitedly and joking as they urged the sailors to lower the boats that would take them to the shore. They jostled and pushed each other in their eagerness to be the first ashore.

Her uncle looked down upon them with disdain. "They're like cattle. They must be herded and guided or they'll injure themselves. They're better off here than ashore. There's nothing ashore save a few miserable huts."

"But, Uncle, look at the hill sides. They're covered with grass and flowers. It's fresh and clean. It's summer. The birds are singing and nesting; the bees are filling their hives; the ants are lively and busy; the animals are caring for their young. Everyone's happy to be alive."

He turned toward her. "Marguerite, you mustn't go ashore."

"Why?"

"You're a young lady. These are men who have not seen a young lady for a long time. It's dangerous."

"But the others are going."

"But the others are peasants. They know how to handle men of their own kind. No, you must stay aboard the ship."

Her eyes sparkled. "Uncle, Old Damienne will be with me. The men won't bother us."

Roberval laughed harshly. "Do you really think Old Damienne will be able to protect you?"

"Uncle, I'm sure nothing will happen to me. I'm as eager to go ashore as anyone else. We've been aboard this ship for two months. You must let me go ashore."

A sailor, barefooted, in torn knee-length breeches with a rope belt, and a dirty tar-stained shirt, ran across the main deck toward the after-deck stairs. He shouted as he ran. "Sieur de Roberval, some fishermen want to see you ashore. Immediately. They say it's very important. Come." As the sailor rushed up to him, Roberval asked, "What seems to be the trouble?"

"Sir, I'm not sure, but there seems to be some sort of dispute between the French fishermen and the Portuguese. The Frenchmen think you may be able to settle it."

Roberval grumbled, "Those Portuguese. They always think that everything belongs to them. I'm sure it has to do with possession of some of the racks...or some of the huts. I'll attend to it."

"Uncle, can I come with you?"

5. Discovery

Old Damienne followed a step behind Marguerite. "Your uncle won't be happy with you. He said you were to stay aboard the ship. He said it was dangerous for you to be ashore."

Marguerite ambled along the rocky beach, picking her way carefully up the steep bank. "My uncle would like me to be a prisoner. He doesn't know how boring life aboard that creaky ship is. He's busy with his affairs."

The men working along the beach nodded their heads in greeting. Some smiled, and some of the younger ones smiled invitingly, but none said anything. Men were throwing reddish-brown codfish with creamy bellies from the heavy planked boats to others on the shore who dropped them into large wooden tubs. When a tub was full, two men grasped the open handholds at the top of the tub and hurried up the bank to a long table where others cut off the heads, gutted them, and split them in two. Then they tossed the prepared fish into another wooden tub that was carried to the racks that scattered the hillside. There, the fish were spread in a single layer and allowed to dry in the sun. Young boys moved among the racks turning the split fish so that both sides dried evenly.

A bass voice called, "Mademoiselle Roberval…Mademoiselle Roberval"

Marguerite looked around, startled. She did not recognize the voice. Old Damienne drew abreast of her and whispered loudly, "Marguerite, it's Robert Le Jeune, Sieur de Montreuil." Marguerite looked about searching for the source of the voice. A young man with dark hair flowing to his shoulders clambered over the rocks leading from the beach. He waved his hand in greeting as he approached.

Marguerite watched him. He was as handsome as she had remembered him. His tall, lean body moved with the grace of a deer, as he hurried toward her.

Before she could greet him, he laughed, showing white, even teeth. "I heard you were with the expedition, and I tried to get messages to you, but I suppose you never received them."

Marguerite stared at him, unsmiling.

"Mademoiselle Roberval, don't you remember me? I'm Robert Le Jeune. We met at Amiens some time ago."

He held in his right hand a tam with a long blue ostrich plume dangling from the left side, and he bowed deeply at the waist.

Marguerite smiled coquetishly and answered softly, "Yes, I remember you, Monsieur Le Jeune."

The next days were exciting for Marguerite. Her uncle was busy trying to settle a dispute between the Portuguese fishermen and their French neighbors. Both claimed they owned a number of racks high on the hillside, and neither would allow the other to use them. Her uncle held many meetings with the fishermen trying to keep the quarrel from erupting into violence.

Each day Old Damienne made sure that Marguerite's uncle was away. Then she and Marguerite were rowed ashore. There, Robert met them, and under Damienne's watchful eye the young couple explored the rocky hills, the streams, and the inlets around the harbor. Their laughter and happiness made her feel young again. She remembered when she and her late husband had discovered each other—the fun they had, the laughter they shared, the jokes they played on each other, the joy they felt in each other's company.

Each morning she helped Marguerite to prepare for her expeditions ashore. She watched as her charge went about her toilet. She listened as Marguerite asked her advice. "Damienne, do you think Robert will like this bonnet? Is my dress the right color? Is my hair in place?"

Damienne looked at her charge. Mademoiselle Marguerite was no beauty, but neither was she ugly. Her dark hair shone: highlights sparkled from the carefully formed curls and ringlets. Her green eyes, almost a pale olive, large and expressive, dominated her fair face. Only one thing kept her from being beautiful—her nose, which was characteristically Roberval, long and thin. It lengthened her face and drew away from her small heart-shaped mouth.

"You're beautiful, my dear."

Marguerite wrinkled her nose as she peered into a small hand mirror. "But does Robert think I'm beautiful?"

Old Damienne smiled. The way Robert pursued Marguerite convinced her that he thought she was beautiful. "I'm sure he does."

There was a knock at the door.

The servant moved quickly to it and asked, "Who's there?"

"I have a message for Miss Roberval."

Damienne lifted the latch and opened the door. A hand passed in a folded sheet of paper. The door closed.

Damienne murmured, "It's from Robert."

Marguerite smiled. "Quick, give it to me."

* * *

Marguerite seized the extended gloved hand that drew her up the steep incline of the point of land. She straightened up, and drew in a deep breath. Then she looked out to sea. The bright sun glinted off the shimmering wavelets like diamonds spread over an azure felt mat. The squawking gulls and gannets wheeled and soared back and forth over the harbor below them.

The tall young man held her hand steadying her as she surveyed the scene below. Boats moved back and forth from the ships anchored in the protected bay, and on shore, men scurried about, some busy with the fish newly arrived from the incoming fishing boats, some with passengers from the three large warships that comprised her uncle's expedition. From the heights they could not hear the shouts and chatter of the people below them.

"Robert, it's a beautiful sight. Maybe Uncle should make this the site of his colony."

Robert laughed. "Fish are not gold and silver and spices. Monsieur Cartier has promised us riches on the site that he has chosen."

Marguerite squeezed his hand. "That's true. Uncle's right. This is nothing but a fishing station."

Robert turned to face Marguerite. He seized her hands in his. "Marguerite, when we get to the colony, we must be married. Monsieur Cartier has priests with him. They can marry us."

She raised herself slowly on tiptoes and kissed him gently on the lips. "Yes, but first we must ask Uncle's permission."

Robert frowned. "That may not be easy, my darling. I don't think your uncle approves of me as a husband." He nodded his head sadly. "I'm not rich enough."

"Robert, I have enough for both of us."

He shook his head. "No, Marguerite, we must wait until I've made my fortune. And your uncle has promised all of us a chance to become wealthy."

"Robert, we can't hide our love forever. We must tell him soon. If he finds out that we are meeting secretly, there's no telling what he'll do. Uncle isn't an easy man. You know that. He's a soldier and he treats everyone as if they were soldiers under his command. We must tell him as soon as possible."

Robert shook his head again. "It's not the time now. He's very busy with the dispute and getting water and other supplies aboard our ships. We must wait."

* * *

Marguerite stood before her uncle. The air was tense and charged.

Roberval looked up at his niece, his face rigid. "What's this that I've heard?" His voice was cold and sharp.

Marguerite opened her mouth to answer, but before she could the older man shouted, "Who gave you permission to see this young upstart? Who arranged for you to meet this fortune seeker?" His face reddened and his voice rose. "You've shamed me. I've treated you like a daughter, but you've deceived me."

"But..."

"Don't interrupt me. I'm your uncle. I'm responsible for you. I'm your guardian. You've disgraced the Roberval name. Running off unchaperoned. Everyone in port knew of you and young Le Jeune. But you failed to inform me."

"But..."

"Don't speak until you're asked to."

"But..."

"You've been meeting this poor young man who's not worthy of your interest, and you've failed to tell me about it. I'm the laughing stock. Everyone knows you're seeing this man...everyone but me. Marguerite, that's not proper. If the young man wished to court you, he should have spoken to me. He didn't. His actions are not honorable."

Marguerite stamped her right foot. "But let me explain."

"My dear, there is nothing to explain. You've been seeing Robert Le Jeune behind my back...without my permission. You've disgraced my good name...your good name. You know, Marguerite, that's not the honorable way to carry out a courtship."

"But, Uncle, listen..."

"I will not listen to a girl who practices deception. If she lies for one thing, she'll lie for others. I can't trust you, my dear niece. I brought you with me to be of help in establishing the new colony, but you're causing problems. You're not helping."

Marguerite stamped her foot again, more firmly. Her voice rose shrilly. "Uncle, you must listen. I'm not one of your officers or soldiers to be ordered about." Her eyes sparkled brightly. Her cheeks flushed. "You will listen to me."

She stepped closer to him and bent down, her face before his. "Robert and I are in love. We want to be married just as soon as possible."

Roberval rose from his chair. He placed both hands atop his cane. "You'll never have my permission to marry that scalawag. He wants only your money and your name. He's not in love with you. You'll never get my permission."

"We're in love, Uncle. We'll marry without your permission. I don't need your permission. I'm of age, and he is too."

His voice was low and menacing. "As long as you're on my ships, I'm in charge. You'll not marry, nor will you see that young man again. You'll be confined to this ship. And your young man will be confined to his ship. You'll not see him again!"

"You can't do that."

"And who's to stop me, my dear. I'm the commander here. I'm the law. You'll be confined to your quarters. There'll be a guard at your door twenty-four hours a day."

"That's ridiculous. You can't keep me on this ship forever. You can't keep us apart forever. When we arrive, you'll have to let us out."

"By then, my dear, I'm sure you'll have seen the error of your ways. By then you'll have forgotten this young foolish man."

Marguerite glared at her uncle. She had heard rumours that he was a difficult man, stern and unbending. She had heard some of the soldiers complain of his strict and cruel orders. She had heard that he expected complete obedience. She had heard also that his punishments were cruel and harsh. The rumours were right.

"I'll never submit to such orders. You've no right to treat me in this way. You've no right to separate me from the man I love. You're afraid that he'll get my money, and you'll be forced to return all the money my father loaned you. Now I understand why you are doing this."

Roberval forced a laugh. "My niece, you're wrong. I've only your happiness in mind. You'd be sorry if you married that man. He's an opportunist, a fortune seeker, a gambler, and an adventurer. He doesn't love you. He sees you as a way to further his own fortunes. My dear, you're a prize catch. You're a Roberval, a courtier, a friend of the king of France."

"That's not true. You're more concerned with your own fortunes than you are of my welfare. We're in love. We'll be married, whether you want it or not."

"Never!"

6. Punishment

The roll of the ship did not cool Marguerite's anger. She had been confined to the small cabin for the past five days. Each day her anger intensified; each day her uncle ignored her. Old Damienne was patient and uncomplaining, but as a servant she was used to the moods and spells of her masters; she accepted these happenings as part of the life of a servant.

Marguerite knew that Commodore Jacques Cartier had arrived in St. John's harbor with a fleet of three ships. She had watched them arrive on the second afternoon of her confinement. She even remembered the name of his flagship, Grande Hermine, with its three masts and its wide square sails. Several times Monsieur Cartier came aboard their ship, and she heard her uncle and the commodore quarreling. At one time she heard her uncle accuse Monsieur Cartier of abandoning his post at the colony headquarters which he had named Charlesbourg Royal in honor of King Francis's son, Charles.

Each day she also quarreled with her uncle. She insisted that she be freed and that she be allowed to see Robert. Even this morning they had argued. As she looked out the open porthole of the small cabin she recalled the incident.

Her uncle was in a foul mood. The evening before, he and Cartier had squabbled again. Cartier wanted to abandon the expedition because he saw no hope of establishing a permanent settlement, as the Indians were no longer friendly. They didn't want the French to establish on their lands. But her uncle had insisted that Cartier return to the settlement that he had built. Cartier refused.

As they ate their breakfast of roasted cod and ship biscuits with red wine, Marguerite asked, "Uncle, you must let me off the ship. You must allow me my freedom."

Roberval glanced up from his plate. "I won't let you out of this room until you promise me that you'll never see that young man again."

Marguerite's face reddened. Her pulse quickened. Each time she asked for her freedom, his answer was always the same. "Uncle, I love Robert. I can't make such a promise. He loves me too. Where is he?"

"He's confined to his quarters."

"Uncle, that's not fair. He isn't to blame."

Her uncle's face twisted into a scowl. His bushy eyebrows twitched, and his thin mustache quivered. "I'll hear no more of this."

"Uncle, I insist that you let me see Robert. You've no right to keep us apart."

"My dear young lady, I have every right to keep you apart. He's not worthy of you. You're under my authority, as commander of this expedition, as your uncle who is your guardian since your father—my brother—and your mother are both dead. You're my responsibility."

Marguerite's voice rose shrilly. "You can never keep us apart. We'll find a way to escape you."

Roberval laughed harshly. "That will be very difficult, my dear. If it's necessary, I'll keep you confined until either of you die." He laughed again, as if taunting her.

"I insist that you free me. I've committed no crime."

Her uncle's dark eyes glittered. "Ah, yes, you have. You've disobeyed my direct orders. You continue to question my authority. You insist that you'll see this young man. You dirty our honorable name. I have every right to keep you confined to these quarters."

She clenched her fists. "I'll find a way to see Robert."

"That will be difficult, my dear. We're under way. We're headed for the Strait of Belle Isle and then we'll enter the Gulf of St. Lawrence."

"You'll never keep us apart forever!"

"My dear, if you insist on this silly romance, I'll take more drastic measures. I'll make sure that you never see this young man again."

The tone of his voice frightened her. She had heard that her uncle could be very cruel. "What do you plan to do?" Her voice trembled.

"If you insist on seeing this man, I'll make sure that you never see him again."

"You can't kill him. He's done nothing wrong. He hasn't disobeyed you."

He laughed. He threw back his head and laughed.

His laughter irritated her, but it also frightened her. "You're right, my dear. I can't kill him. But I can banish him from my expedition. He's a disruptive force. He's a danger to me...and to you. If you insist on this foolish behavior, I'll abandon him on one of these islands."

Later that day, Old Damienne, carrying a wooden bucket of water, entered the tiny cabin. Her face looked worried.

"Damienne, what is the matter? You don't look very happy."

"It's bad news, Mademoiselle."

"What is it?"

"I think Monsieur Roberval is going to carry out his threat. I overheard him talking with the captain."

"What was he saying. Quick, you must tell me."

"He told the captain to have the lookout find a suitable island along these shores."

"A suitable island for what?"

"Of that, I'm not sure, but I overheard the quarrel with your uncle this morning. He threatened to maroon Robert to keep you and him separated."

Marguerite laughed. "You don't think he was serious, do you?"

Damienne did not smile. Her face remained sober and worried. "Your uncle isn't a man to antagonize. He expects everyone to obey him. His anger's well known among his servants and those under him."

"But, Damienne, he's just."

Damienne looked at Marguerite quizzically, as if she didn't believe that.

"But, Damienne, he's just. I'm sure he wouldn't do anything that serious."

Damienne shrugged her shoulders. "He's had many men flogged for minor infractions of his rules. Marguerite, can't you see that your uncle can be very cruel?"

"But those men deserved their punishment. They were guilty. Robert's done nothing wrong."

"In your eyes he's done nothing wrong. But your uncle believes that both of you are guilty of disobeying his authority…that Robert's been as much to blame as you have. He doesn't want to punish you any more than he has to, so Robert must bare the brunt of his wrath."

Marguerite gazed out the left porthole. Off to the west she could see the hazy outline of the coast. They were sailing close to the shore. Maybe Old Damienne was right. Why else would they be sailing so close to the shore? But there were many reasons. The area they were sailing into was little known although many fishing boats fished in these waters. The charts for this area were scarce and incomplete. She opened the porthole. A breeze entered and cooled her face. The salt air was refreshing. She heard the shouts of sailors as they went about their work, calling instructions to each other. The creak of the ship's timbers, the squeal of the wooden pulleys, the snap of the full sails, told her that they were making good way.

She heard the shout from the crow's nest. "Captain, a large island off the port bow."

She did not understand the muffled response, as the fresh breeze seemed to carry it out to sea. But she did notice a renewed effort as the sailors scurried to obey captain's commands as relayed by the mate.

She looked to the southwest. A league away she could see the full sails of the other two ships in the flotilla. They were following her uncle's flagship closely.

The ship slowed as the sailors reduced sail. The two following ships were doing the same thing. They were coming about and heading toward the hazy shoreline. What was happening? Why were they sailing toward the shore? Was Old Damienne right? Did her uncle plan to maroon Robert on one of the offshore islands as Damienne had reported to her?

Her heartbeat quickened. Her palms felt moist. She didn't know what to think. Her uncle had always been kind and treated her almost as a daughter. But now, if he planned to abandon Robert on one of these deserted islands, he was being cruel, cruel to her, and cruel to her lover.

"Damienne, we're slowing down. We've turned toward the shore. The other ships are following us. What's happening?"

"My dear, I don't know. Maybe what I heard is true."

Marguerite swung around to face the narrow, low door that lead to the poopdeck. "I must speak to my uncle. I must find out what's happening."

She spurted across the room and seized the metal latch of the door. She tried to twist it, but it was locked. She tugged at it; she twisted it again, but it would not move. She shouted, "Let me out! Uncle, I must speak to you. Open this door."

Only the creaking sounds of the moving ship responded to her shouts.

She leaned against the door and beat it with clenched fists, crying, "I must see my uncle. Open this door. It's an emergency."

She stopped, listening. She heard the scuff of feet. Then silence.

She pounded again. She rattled the latch. She pounded again. She cried out. "Open this door. I must see my uncle."

To her surprise, the latch turned and the door opened. Her uncle stood framed in the doorway.

A wicked grin hovered around his mouth. His eyes glittered. He stared at his niece. Then he laughed. "We've found just the place for your lover."

Marguerite glared up into his face. The satisfaction she saw there made her heart skip a beat.

"You'll never see your lover again."

"Uncle, what's happening? What are you doing?"

He bowed at the waist and swept his hand outward from the cabin door. "Come, you'll see."

Marguerite hesitated. She felt as if something evil was about to happen. She felt crushed and powerless. Her knees shook. Her face paled. She moved swiftly ahead of her uncle. She followed his pointing finger toward the steps leading to the high poop deck. Quickly she climbed the steep steps. Roberval followed close behind her.

She moved to the port rail and looked toward the other ships. They had slowed and stopped, as had their ship. Their sails hung limp and empty of wind, heading into it. She looked to her left. They were in a large cove. Its waters were smooth and calm, protected from the fresh breeze that stirred the waters to white-capped waves farther out to sea.

Ahead she could sea a rocky coastline, and rising from a narrow beach, high cliffs with a multitude of seabirds squawking and mewling as they soared and dove, weaving and whirling in great flocks. The closer they came to shore, the louder the raucous sounds became. The cliffs seemed covered with roosting birds, some in repose, others fighting for a place on the rock ledges.

Behind the steep cliffs, she saw the dark firs, pines, and spruces covering the hills like green fur. Light grassy meadows stood out against the dark green of the forests.

The ships coasted closer to the shore, and stopped short as the anchors took hold.

"Uncle, why are we stopping here?"

"My dear, I told you. After today, you'll never see your lover again. He'll not bother you again."

"What will you do?"

He laughed. "Robert's been difficult. He's been a bad influence on the others. He spreads false rumours. He disrupts the good attitude of the rest of the colonists. I can't have that. He'll not change, therefore he's left me little choice."

Her voice trembled. "What will happen to him?"

He laughed again. "We'll put him ashore on that island. If he's lucky, he won't be there for long. A fishing boat will find him and take him off. If he's not lucky..." His voice trailed off.

"Uncle, you can't do that. That's unjust. That's inhuman."

Her uncle raised his hand and pointed to the nearest ship. A boat was being lowered.

"Who'll be with him?"

Roberval shrugged his shoulders. "No one."

She watched in silence, grimly as the boat bobbed beside the ship. She watched as several bundles and packages were passed down to four sailors in the boat. She watched Robert Le Jeune moved slowly down the ladder on the side of the ship to the boat below.

She turned to her uncle, her eyes flashing. "I'll tell everyone of your cruelty...of your injustice...of your savagery. I'll be more dangerous to you than Robert ever was!"

7. Banished

"Uncle, you can't put him on that island alone. He'll be driven crazy by the loneliness. You must leave someone with him."

"I can't do that. Besides, no one wants to go with him."

"I'll go with him."

Roberval looked at her, shocked. "You're not serious."

"Yes, I am. Send me to the island also."

"My dear, that's out of the question. That's the most stupid thing that I've heard. You have your duty. You're my niece. You must support me. You must be sensible and act like a courtier, not like some undisciplined peasant."

"Uncle, if you don't change your mind and bring Robert back, I'll cause you a great deal of trouble." Her eyes sparkled with anger.

Roberval stared at his niece. She wasn't acting like a sensible noble woman. She was letting her heart get in the way of her reasoning. Robert Le Jeune was a handsome young man, charming and well-bred, but he was poor. His family was poor and not very well connected. There was rumour at the court that they had opposed the king in his wars with Netherlands. Why was she behaving in such a stubborn and abrasive manner?

He tried to reason with her. "My dear, you must forget Robert Le Jeune. He isn't an appropriate husband for you. He has no connections at the court; he's impoverished. His family's old, but they haven't managed their affairs well. He can't help you in any way."

"Uncle, I know all that. But you forget one important thing: we love each other. Money and property are not the only important things in this world: love is. The church teaches us that without love we are nothing.

Christ told us to love one and other. That's the most important thing in life. I love Robert and he loves me."

Roberval laughed. "That's not love, my dear. That's foolishness. That's not the kind of love that Jesus had in mind."

Her eyes narrowed. Her flushed cheeks quivered. She clenched her fists. Would her uncle ever understand that she loved Robert and wanted to be with him? She would comfort him and help him in every hardship. "You don't understand. You're a selfish man. You want everything your way. But you can't have everything your way. Commodore Jacques Cartier realized that, and he disobeyed your orders. He's gone back to France."

Jacques Cartier's departure to France against his orders had reduced his authority. Even his niece would not listen to him. Others in his group were complaining and rebellion might break out at any moment. "Marguerite, I won't argue with you any more. I've made my decision and I must stick by it. Robert Le Jeune will be placed on that island. His survival will depend on him. I'm sending him there with supplies and tools. If he's lucky, fishermen will soon find him, if not, he'll have to learn to live off the land…like the Indians."

"You can't do that, Uncle. He's done nothing to deserve such a fate. I'm the one who should be sent to that island. I'm the one who displeases you. I'm the one that disobeyed your silly rules. So you must send me to the island…not Robert."

"No!'

"You must. If you don't send me to the island, I'll cause much more trouble than Robert will. I'll cause trouble with the sailors…the soldiers…and the other colonists." He laughed, but it was a quiet, tentative laugh. "My dear niece, you can do nothing to harm me. If necessary, I'll keep you confined to your quarters until you change your mind."

Her voice rose shrilly. "I'll never change my mind. I love Robert. I'll always love him. You can never change my mind."

Several sailors paused in their work and stared up at the high poopdeck. Marguerite's high-pitched voice caught their attention. They sympathized with the young woman. Sieur Roberval was a hard man. He punished severely anyone that crossed him. The story of Marguerite and Robert Le Jeune was well known throughout the expedition. Everyone liked the young couple, particularly young Robert, who treated everyone as a friend.

Marguerite walked across the long, narrow deck toward the stairs that lead to the quarterdeck. She stopped at the rail to the left of the stairs and surveyed the main deck. Several people—some sailors, some soldiers, and some ordinary colonists—who were enjoying the fine weather, watched her curiously. She pointed toward the longboat that was being rowed toward the nearby island. "My uncle is abandoning the man I love on that island." Her voice rose. Her uncle stood stunned, his face blank. His eyes opened in surprise. His mouth tensed. His eyes stared. Why was his niece being so difficult? Why couldn't she see the situation his way?

He strode across the deck, his heavy shoes clumping noisily on the thick planks. He grabbed her by the arm and whirled her toward him.

She gasped in pain as his fingers squeezed her upper arm.

He snarled, "My dear, I've been very patient with you. I've tried to reason with you. But you won't listen. You're as bad as that young man that I've banished from this expedition. If you weren't my niece, my flesh and blood, I'd punish you in the same way, but first I'd have you flogged like a common peasant for your unruly and unbecoming behavior."

Her eyes opened wide in surprise and pain. Slowly she recovered and her eyes glittered. Her voice was ice. "Take your hands off me." She did not yell or scream.

He shook her vigorously; her dark ringlets swung back and forth.

She jerked her arms from his grasp. "Don't ever touch me again, dear uncle. I'm not one of your soldiers or your servants to be ordered about. You owe me. I don't owe you. I have a contract with you. I've loaned you money. I have your notes. Remember, we're partners. I command you to release Robert and return him to his ship. If you don't..."

His face flushed. His thin mustache quivered. His hands dropped to his side. His voice was low and menacing. "If you don't stop this exhibition, I'll have you tied and muzzled."

Her dark eyes flashed. "You wouldn't dare!"

"My dear niece, do not tempt me."

Old Damienne stepped to her side. "Miss Marguerite, maybe you better think about what your uncle says." She placed her hand gently on Marguerite's arm.

Marguerite shook her arm dislodging the servant's.

"Uncle, you'll never get away with this. When I return to France I'll appeal to the king. Robert is a nobleman. He has the right to a trial." She turned to face the main deck where a group of people had gathered, watching the dispute that was taking place on the poopdeck. Some smiled in amusement, others muttered their support for Marguerite, a few noisily agreed with Marguerite that Roberval was treating the young man unjustly. "My uncle is punishing Robert Le Jeune because he's angry at me."

Most nodded their heads affirmatively; some grumbled under their breath; one or two shouted support.

Roberval stepped to the rail. "Friends, this young lady, my niece, has disobeyed me. That young man has also caused me great concern because he has refused to obey my orders. I cannot tolerate people who cause us trouble. We must work together. We are coming to this land to seek our fortunes—to find gold, and diamonds, and spices. We can only succeed if we work together...without quarreling. But my niece will not listen to that. She thinks she can do as she pleases, but you know that none of us can. We must help each other if we are to become wealthy. Monsieur Cartier has abandoned us, because he has found gold and diamonds. He has taken his wealth and returned to France, but we must go on and get our share."

The grumbles turned to shouts of agreement. The glum faces turned to smiles. People turned to each other and agreed.

Marguerite watched the sudden change of attitude with disbelief. Moments earlier they had supported her. Now their greed had turned them against her.

Her uncle continued, "My niece is trying to destroy our chance at wealth. She's trying to make you believe that this expedition is doomed. She's trying to cause a rift between you and me. You know that without me, we cannot succeed. I'm your commander, your leader, appointed by your king. Do you want to listen to a silly girl who has only her welfare and that of her lover on her mind?"

The low murmur turned to a rumble. Some shouted their support, others laughed their approval, all agreed with the commander. Someone shouted, "Send her to the island with her lover." Another took up the idea. "Yes, let her go and comfort him." Still another said, "We don't need her to find gold. Banish her."

"My uncle is not concerned with your fortunes. He's concerned with his. He'll use you. He needs you more than you need him."

Someone shouted, "We need him more than we need you."

Roberval looked at his niece; a sly smile moved his lips. He spoke softly, almost a whisper, "You see, my dear, greed is stronger than any emotion."

"You're a monster. I'll sue you when I get back to France. I'll ruin you."

"No, my dear, you will not." His voice was ominous. "You love your young nobleman. Then you can join him. I can't tolerate your continued disobedience and insolence. You'll disrupt the harmony of this expedition. I've decided. You'll join your lover!"

8. The Island

Marguerite watched wistfully as the two longboats moved farther and farther from the shore back to the waiting ships. She seethed with anger and muttered under her breath as she berated her uncle. Robert stood to her right, his left arm across her shoulders, staring silently as the boats became small specks on the clear, calm ocean. Old Damienne stood behind the pair, tears in her eyes, as she clasped a knitted shawl about her thin, stooped shoulders.

Marguerite's jaw muscles tensed. "I'll make my uncle pay for this if it's the last thing I do. He has no authority to do this." Her voice trembled with anger, but it was strong and irrepressible.

Robert looked down at her. "My love, we won't be here long. Many boats fish in these waters. I'm sure other ships will be along in a few days. We'll be rescued."

Old Damienne moved beside Marguerite. "I hope we're still alive when the fishermen come. Did you hear what one of the sailors said?" Her voice quavered.

Robert turned to her quickly. "No. What did he say?"

"He said this island was inhabited by demons. That's why the Sieur chose it. That's why the fishermen avoid it. He said the demons would devour us, and we'd be no more bother for Monsieur Roberval."

Marguerite turned abruptly toward the older woman. "Damienne, you can't listen to every rumour you hear." She looked around. Steep cliffs rose from the narrow rocky beach on which they stood. The sailors had deposited them and their small cargo of supplies on the first convenient landing place they could find. Hurriedly they had unloaded the baggage and the few tools that her uncle had sent with them. And quickly they had returned to the ship. Maybe what Old Damienne said was true; the sailors had wasted little time on the island. She looked up to the high cliffs that rose from the beach. The rocks rose almost perpendicular from the beach, and the clefts were covered with the nests of sea birds—gulls, gannets, other birds she did not know—that screeched and squawked as they flew about them. Some dived toward them, narrowly missing them as they tried to persuade them to leave.

Robert muttered, "Even the birds don't want us."

Old Damienne raised her hands to protect her head as a particularly irate gannet dived at her. She shouted above the birds' screeches, "These birds will kill us. We can't stay here." Her voice shook and she sounded as if she was about to break into tears.

"Damienne, you're right. We must find a better place to set up camp." Marguerite placed her arm around the old servant's shoulders. Poor Damienne, she thought, you had nothing to do with this, but you've been punished with us. Her uncle was most unfair. The old servant had not made a fuss when her uncle ordered her to accompany Marguerite. Marguerite was grateful that the old woman had agreed to come with her. It would be comfortable to have the old servant's company. "Don't be afraid. If there are demons on this island, we'll have the Lord's protection."

At that moment a quavering scream echoed along the cliffs, shrill and piercing. They stared blankly up the long cleft walls trying to locate the source of the discordant sound.

Robert whispered, "My God, what was that?"

Marguerite lifted her right hand to shade her eyes as she searched the rock walls for the origin of the sound. All she could see was the raucous activity of the thousands of nesting birds.

Old Damienne shrilled, "That's one of the demons that lives on this island." Her voice trailed off. "That's why it's called the 'Isle of Demons'. They'll get us and devour us." Her voice lowered to a hoarse rasp.

Marguerite spoke out. "We can't spend the rest of our days huddled here on the beach. If there are demons, only the Lord can protect us. Let's find a place to spend the night. Maybe a ship will come by tomorrow and we'll be gone from this forsaken place."

Robert nodded his head and moved along the base of the cliff searching for a way to the top. Off to his right he noticed at stream running down through the rocks and trickling into the wavelets along the shore. He rushed to it, knelt on a rock, and scooped some of the water to his mouth. It was fresh and clear and cold. Its sweetness satisfied his thirst. His eyes followed the stream up the incline. Although it was steep, he felt they would be able to follow the stream bank to the top of the cliffs.

He called to the women, "I think I've found a way to the top. I'll follow this stream and see if it goes to the top." He hurried, scrambling over the rocks and boulders that bordered the gurgling stream.

* * *

Darkness descended upon the camp they had set up in a grove of tall pines and spruces. During the remaining hours of the afternoon they carried to the crest of the jagged cliffs the few things they needed to establish a temporary camp.

Marguerite insisted that the first thing they needed was a fire placed on the highest point along that shore to serve as a beacon for any ships that might come by. She convinced Robert that it would not only serve as a signal for ships, but it would also protect them from any wild animals or demons that might be lurking about.

Throughout the afternoon they labored. While Robert collected firewood, she and Old Damienne made several trips to the beach to haul the things they most needed—food, for they were hungry, blankets to protect them from the chill night air, and a piece of heavy sailcloth to serve as a makeshift shelter. She knew that rain and fog were common along these shores. Although the weather was bright, she knew that it could change in minutes.

The fading rays of the sun glowed dimly in the western skies, but they were ready for the night. Twice they heard the terrible screech that had frightened them on the beach, and each time they were unable to discover where the sound came from and what might be causing it. Each time Old Damienne insisted it was the demons that haunted the island.

That first night was one that Marguerite would never forget. The darkness enveloped them so deeply that she thought she had gone blind. No moon glowed, no stars shone; blackness reigned. Throughout the night the noise of the birds diminished, but did not die away completely, and other sounds rose—shrieks, screams, moans, groans, bellows, and blasts. She was sure the island must be the home of a thousand demons. Even Robert was uneasy, and Old Damienne cried out in fright as the loudest sounds rumbled through the darkness; Marguerite could hear her praying and pleading with God to protect them.

Dawn came slowly. The bright sunshine of the previous day was replaced by a dull grey overcast, and a cool wind from the sea brought squalls of rain. Their sailcloth shelter protected them; their night fears vanished, and they slept late. Hunger finally forced them from the warmth of their beds.

Later that day the sunshine returned; the skies cleared, the birds wheeled noisily overhead, and the breezes lightened. Together they worked at making their camp more comfortable. While Robert rekindled the beacon fire and worked at cutting dead trees for firewood, Marguerite sent Old Damienne to sit by the beacon and watch the seas for a ship. They decided that they must have someone as a lookout at all times; they would take turns watching from the high point of land. Marguerite gathered stones and constructed a crude fireplace where she could hang the pots and set the pans for cooking. She knew that she would have to learn how to cook because she could not depend on her servant to do all the chores that needed to be done. As well, she built a low wall of rocks around the east, north, and west sides of the sailcloth shelter. It kept out the wind and held the canvas firmly, preventing it from blowing away.

As they ate lunch of salt meat and hard ship biscuits, she looked at the small pile of supplies that her uncle had sent—two hogsheads of coarse flour, one of salt pork, another of salted fish, and a small cask of salt as well as a dozen bottles of dark red wine. It wouldn't last long.

"Robert, if a ship doesn't come soon we'll run out of food."

Robert glanced at the small store. "Yes, it won't last long, but there's a good supply of birds' eggs." He grinned at her and looked toward the crest of the cliffs where gulls wheeled and squawked.

Old Damienne glanced up at Marguerite. "I don't think we need worry about food. I saw some porcupines along the edge of the woods, and soon there'll be many berries. There are great clumps of bushes along the edge of the forest."

"I'm sure we'll see a ship soon." Robert smiled with encouragement. "Then we can forget about the demons here. Did you hear them last night, shrieking and screaming?"

"Of course, I heard them. But I prayed and the Lord answered my prayers. They didn't harm us."

Old Damienne's eyes narrowed. "Maybe they'll get us tonight. I've never heard such fierce noises in my life. It sounded as if they came from hell."

Marguerite laughed. "They were bad, but not that bad, and our prayers were stronger. We're here. We're well. We're safe."

Robert lifted his hand toward the sea, and pointed. "What's that off to the right? Is it a sail? Is it a ship?" He rose and hurried to the crest of the cliff.

Marguerite and the old lady followed. They stood staring out to sea. The bright sunlight sparkled on the shifting waves, moving and flickering. The sounds of the screaming birds mingled with the waves washing against the rocky beach.

Robert pointed to his right. Far out a white veil rose from the waters. "It's a sail. There's a ship out there!"

Marguerite shaded her eyes with her right hand. She could see nothing. "Damienne, do you see it. I don't"

The old servant squinted and stuck her head forward as if to bring her closer to the object she was looking for. Then she shook her head slowly. "There's no ship out there."

"Yes, there is. Look, I see it again. To the right. A whitish sail."

Marguerite saw it. A cone shaped wisp of whitish haze. Then it was gone. Then she saw it again. Then she laughed. Her hand dropped to her side, and she turned toward Robert. "That's not a ship. That's a pod of whales. What you see is the steam as they blow." She laughed again, hollowly.

Robert stood rigid, staring at what he had seen. Now he could see the dark humps of several whales and the white steam as they blew water in spouts. Marguerite was right. They were whales frolicking offshore. He tried to hide his disappointment, but he could not. "I was so sure they were ships."

During the next days they kept their watch on the sea, but they didn't even see another pod of whales. The effort of keeping a beacon fire going was too much, so they let it die, but they kept it ready to be lighted if they should spot a ship.

The weather continued warm and sunny. They explored the cliffs and the neighboring woods. They went for long rambles along the coast, exploring. Old Damienne remained behind in the camp on the lookout, ready to light the beacon fire if she should see a ship. Robert set snares and traps in the nearby woods to catch some of the small animals that lived there—rabbits, squirrels, and porcupines. Marguerite gathered eggs from the nearby nests and berries from the nearby bushes. The wild flowers bloomed turning their world into a fairyland of colours and fragrances.

Hand in hand, Marguerite and Robert spent their afternoons roaming about the island. One time they came upon a herd of seals that splashed into the water and disappeared in the sparkling waves of the ocean. Another time they saw a large iceberg float by like a fantasy island, its spires like those of a castle, but white and blue and green, and when the sun shone on parts of it, it reflected back a rainbow of colours.

The days turned into weeks. But no ships came.

The summer days shortened. Each day they looked anxiously toward the sea; each day ended in disappointment. Yet Robert and Marguerite were happy. Their love blossomed and bore fruit just like the wild berries and cherries that flourished in the woods surrounding their camp.

Early one morning as the grey light of dawn filtered into their camp, Marguerite was awakened by a noise—a noise different from the usual screams and shrieks that filled the night. She rubbed her sleep-filled eyes and slowly raised her head, scanning the open area before their sailcloth tent.

A grunt like that of a pig came to her, not more than ten yards away. She froze, scanning the area, but she saw nothing. Slowly she lifted herself to her elbow. The grunting sounds increased in intensity and frequency. She was sure there were no pigs on the island. Although Robert and she had not explored every corner of the island, she felt sure that if there were pigs she would have seen some evidence of them.

Her heart started to beat rapidly. What if it was one of the demons that Old Damienne believed lived on the island? She heard a scraping sound, as if someone was digging. Then a boulder crashed against another. Her eyes followed the sound.

In the dim light she could see a large white mass moving. The grunts and groans emitted from it. The form was digging at the hole in which they cached their salt pork and bottles of wine. She watched as the animal tore at the boulders and stones that they used as a cover for the cache.

She reached for the blunderbuss that Robert kept loaded at all times. Although it was primed, she knew that it was useless unless she could light the corded match that hung from its holder. Fire from that match was the only way to discharge the weapon. To light it she had to crawl to the banked fire in the stone fire pit, uncover a glowing coal, light the end of the cordlike match, and then she would be ready to face the large animal that had invaded their camp. Robert and Old Damienne still slept, loud snores emitting from the old lady's mouth. She made more noise than the demons of the night.

Slowly Marguerite pushed back the covers and with the heavy gun in her left hand she slithered toward the fire pit a few feet before the shelter. She watched the white animal as it struggled with the boulders, sniffing and snuffing as it got nearer the cached foodstuffs.

Once it raised its head, waving it back and forth, scenting the air. Marguerite froze. When the animal returned to its digging, she moved forward.

The animal looked like a bear, but it was the largest bear that she had ever seen—and it was white. There were no bears like that in France.

She reached the fire pit. She brushed the piled ashes with her hand feeling for the hot coals that she knew were buried deep within. A glow appeared, and she touched the twisted rope to the ember. A wisp of smoke ascended, and the acrid smell of the burning fibers drifted to her nose.

Instantly, the large animal's head jerked upward. It extended its nose into the air, sniffing. Then it swung around to face her.

She rose to her knees, lifting the heavy weapon to face the huge animal. As she moved, the animal roared. The sound reverberated through the still air. She heard Old Damienne scream. She heard Robert shout. But she did not take her eyes off the animal.

It shook its head from side to side. It lowered it to the ground, searching. Its small eyes gleamed. It took a step forward. Old Damienne screamed again. Then the animal moved toward them increasing its speed as it loped.

Ten feet away it stopped, rose on its hind legs, and roared again. Marguerite could see the vastness of its open maw, the gleaming yellow teeth, the dark pink of its gums, and its foaming slather.

She tried to raise the gun, to point it at the broad chest, but it was very heavy. She sat down, drew up her left knee, and rested the gun on it. She sighted along the flaring barrel. The bell of the barrel covered the upper part of the animal. With her right hand she touched the glowing end of the cord to the firing hole.

The concussion of the exploding powder threw her backwards. The gun was torn from her grip and fell beside her. The animal roared; the sound echoed over the cliffs. It dropped to its four feet and moved toward her. She screamed. She scrambled to her feet.

She saw the blood flowing from the animal's mouth. Its eyes glistened viciously. Then it crashed at her feet. The hulk shuddered. A swishing sound of escaping air issued from its mouth, and a froth of pink foam ballooned from each nostril. The eyes closed. The animal quit moving.

9. Tragedy

Autumn colours dotted the landscape. Nights became cooler and shorter. There were no more eggs in the nests. Birds were leaving the island.

After they recovered from the shock of the bear attack, Marguerite insisted that they build a better, more permanent shelter, so in the days that followed they cut trees from the nearby forest and built a small but sturdy log cabin. The women helped Robert move the heavy logs into place and to chink the holes between them with moss and mud.

One morning, Marguerite awoke feeling sick; her vision blurred, and the scent of food nauseated her. She told her troubles to Old Damienne who only smiled knowingly and whispered to her, "My dear, it will pass. Just rest for a little while and you'll be fine."

"I've never been sick before. Why am I sick now?"

Damienne smiled again. "My dear, I'm sure you know why you're sick?"

Marguerite gasped.

Old Damienne nodded her head gravely. "Yes, my dear, I think you're going to have a baby.

Marguerite looked up to where Robert was placing a log of wood into the stone and mud fireplace along the north wall of the small cabin. She smiled tenderly. She was sure he would be pleased to know that soon he would be a father. She smiled at Old Damienne. "Yes, Damienne, I think you're right."

She did not tell Robert immediately that she was expecting a baby. She wanted to wait until the right moment; she wanted it to be a surprise, a pleasant one.

Later that afternoon as they walked through the woods searching for late berries and acorns, they stopped beside a small stream that gurgled merrily to join another nearby larger stream. The leaves of the sumachs that bordered the tiny stream were mature and red, and songbirds chirped cheerily from their hidden haunts.

Marguerite turned to Robert. "This summer has been the happiest of my life. I love you, Robert. This island is just like heaven."

Robert smiled at her. "My darling, I'm glad you think so. I've found it a little less than heaven. It's been hard work—finding enough food, building a safe home, keeping watch for ships, and protecting ourselves from wild animals. Other than that, it has been pleasant." He twisted his lips wryly. "But I hope we'll be rescued before the ships return to France for the season."

Marguerite knew that the fishing fleets came to this new found land each year to fish for cod in the shallows or banks offshore. She also knew that soon these fleets would be preparing to return home for the winter. During the entire summer they had not seen a single ship although they had kept watch faithfully. Old Damienne was sure that the fishermen were afraid to come near this island, for they, like she, believed that demons inhabited the island. Recently she seemed more comfortable because she no longer mentioned the demons.

"If no ship comes, what'll we do, Robert?"

He shook his head. "We'll prepare for winter. We'll cut wood for the fireplace. We'll increase our supply of fish. We'll gather all the berries we can."

She was pleased with his optimism. She knew they needn't worry about food—fish were plentiful in the bay and in the streams; rabbits and hares and other small animals were easy to catch in the woods; berries and other fruits hung heavy on the branches and bushes. Their small house needed little work to be warm and comfortable. They could survive the winter.

She touched his arm. "Robert, I've a secret to tell you."

He stopped and looked at her tenderly. "How can you keep a secret from me. We're together all the time."

She smiled up at him. She teased, "You don't know everything."

He drew her into his arms. "Quick, tell me. What's your secret?"

She kissed him. "Robert, I'm going to have a baby. Before the year is out you'll be a father. I'll be a mother."

His mouth dropped open. His face drained of color. He stammered, "How will we care for a baby in this God-forsaken land. Who'll help you when it's time to have the baby?" His face looked worried.

Marguerite felt her heart sink. She had expected Robert to be happy and excited, but instead he sounded disappointed and worried. She tried to reassure him. "Robert, you needn't worry about that. Old Damienne has seen many babies come into the world. She knows what to do."

He shook his head in bewilderment. If a ship did not rescue them, the baby would be another responsibility. He hated the loneliness, and the constant tension, the fear of wild animals and injuries and sickness. There was no one to help them. They were alone.

"But a baby'll be another person to protect and feed. A baby here in this wilderness, at this time, is the worst possible happening."

Marguerite dropped her eyes to hide her disappointment. She had hoped that he would be happy at the news as Damienne had been. She realized that nothing she could say would change the way Robert felt. "I'm sorry you're unhappy, Robert. I know a baby's a new responsibility, but I'm sure we'll be rescued before the baby comes."

"And if we're not?"

She lifted her head. "We've been happy this summer. Life's been good. Food's been plentiful. The land's provided. I'm sure it'll be the same this winter if no ship comes."

He looked at her angrily. "Marguerite, I'm tired of this place. I'm tired of just you and the old lady. I'm tired of the birds and their infernal noises. I'm tired of the constant work—gathering wood, fishing, hunting...work, work, work. That's all we do!"

She looked at him carefully. He did look tired. His hair was long and disheveled. His face was thin and drawn. His eyes were dull and tired-looking. The wilderness was depressing him.

During the next weeks, Marguerite watched as Robert became more depressed. Each morning he complained about the lateness of the sunrise as the days became shorter; he grumbled about the need to re-stoke the fire; he muttered about the sameness of their food; and he glumly went about the chores that had to be done: replenishing the wood supply, filling the water buckets, cleaning ashes from the fireplace, and checking the traps set for the small animals. He seldom laughed or smiled any more.

Each day he trudged to the top of the cliff and stood looking out to sea, searching the far horizon for a ship's sail, but none came. She tried to cheer him; sometimes she helped him check the traps that he had set; often she stood by him as they gazed out over the foggy waters. As summer waned, the weather became cooler, and dark grey clouds drifted in from the northwest. Large flocks of birds flew south—geese, ducks, and swans. The leaves of the deciduous trees turned from brilliant green to bright hues of red, yellow, and orange. And then they started to fall.

Each day Marguerite felt heavier and clumsier as the child grew within her. Robert never mentioned the baby, and this saddened her, although Old Damienne was pleased about the coming child.

One morning in late November, after a cold windy night in which a scattering of snow covered the ground, Robert could not rise from his bed. He moaned and groaned but did not speak. Fear clutched at Marguerite's heart.

Old Damienne checked him: She placed her gnarled right hand on his forehead and shook her head slowly. "He has a fever," she muttered.

"Is he very sick?"

She shook her head again. "I don't think so. He has a flu. He must stay in bed for a few days, drink lots of water, eat chicken soup."

"But we don't have chickens."

Old Damienne smiled at Marguerite's worried tone. "We have ducks and geese. They're just as good." And she busied herself at the fireplace preparing the remedy that she had prescribed.

But it did not help. In the days that followed, Robert's fever increased, and he moaned and groaned more. Sometimes his body was covered with sweat; at other times it was hot and dry. Marguerite hovered over him, feeding him and bathing him with wet clothes, but nothing seemed to help.

One morning, he awoke his eyes bright. He raised his head from the down pillow of the crude bed that he had fashioned of poles along the north wall. He called softly, "Marguerite, are you there?"

She hurried to his side. "Yes, Robert, I'm here." She grasped his hand. It was cool and clammy. The bones stuck out like dry sticks. She placed her right hand on his head. It was still warm, but she thought the fever had broken. She was sure he would now recover. She turned to Old Damienne. "Look, Robert is awake. His fever is gone. He'll soon be well."

Old Damienne stared at him from across the room, but she said nothing.

Robert's hand tightened on Marguerite's. "I'm sorry I was so displeased about the child, my darling. I know it'll be a joy to you."

Marguerite frowned. He was talking as if he would not be around when the child arrived. "It will make you happy too."

He sighed deeply. "No, my darling, I won't be around to see the child."

She clasped his hand more tightly. "Robert, you mustn't talk like that. You'll soon be well."

"No, my darling." His voice faded to a whisper. "Kiss me."

She bent over him and her lips brushed his. They were dry and hot. His eyes closed, his body shuddered and went limp.

* * *

Marguerite and Old Damienne buried Robert in a shallow grave on the high point of the cliff where they kept a lookout for ships. After they covered the body with the gravelly clay, they prayed over the grave. Only then did Marguerite cry, the tears rolling down her cheeks as she whispered the Lord's Prayer. Old Damienne stood with her head bowed as the wind whipped her long skirt. The remaining birds screeched and wheeled about them, and the waves thundered against the rocky shore singing a mournful dirge.

The season was late. Soon the winter storms would be upon them covering the land with snow. They had little time for mourning. Each day they added to the growing woodpile; each day they increased their food supply; each day they kept an eye on the sea, hoping for a ship. But none came.

As Marguerite's body swelled, she became more awkward and clumsy, but she was no longer sick in the mornings.

Old Damienne nattered at her to do less, but Marguerite only smiled and said, "If we have to spend the winter here, we must be prepared."

Old Damienne nodded because she knew Marguerite was right.

One afternoon in late November, the grey skies darkened more and a cold wind came from the northwest. The clouds scudded across the sky churning like a boiling cauldron. Marguerite stood at the door of their tiny cabin and remarked, "It smells like snow. I think winter's arrived."

Old Damienne, who stood beside, shrugged her shoulders and replied, "Marguerite, I think you're right. I've seen clouds like that before back home in Picardy."

Marguerite smiled. They were a long way from the pleasant fields of Picardy. The Isle of Demons wasn't like Picardy at all: it was barren, and rocky, and uninhabited—except for the demons that screeched from the woods on dark nights.

A sharp gust of wind swung the door toward her. Tiny particles of ice from shattered snowflakes prickled her face. She latched the crude door and turned to the glowing fire in the fireplace. "At least we'll be warm here." She looked at the large pile of wood that she and her servant had piled against the wall.

Then she felt a sharp pain. She gasped and grasped her stomach. Her brow wrinkled in pain. Old Damienne rushed toward her and helped her to the crude bunk along the wall. Marguerite cried out again. "I think...my time has...come."

"Hush, my child, we'll see."

The next morning, Marguerite lay in bed half-asleep. The birth of her child had taken most of the night, and she remembered Old Damienne hovering over her, comforting her and encouraging her.

Marguerite turned on her right side and stared at the tiny bundle that lay beside her. As she moved, the old lady stirred from the pile of blankets on the floor where she had dozed. She rose quickly and came to the bed. She looked tired, but she smiled, pleased. "It's a beautiful baby girl...healthy...and hungry."

Marguerite sighed happily and drew the child toward her. She drew back the coverlet and stared down at the dark head. Her heart swelled with love. Her hand trembled as she touched the soft, smooth cheek. Now she must survive. She must be strong and protect this baby from the terrors of this new land—the demons, the weather, the wild animals, and any other danger that might threaten them. She drew the child toward her and kissed it tenderly.

10. Resolve

December was a cold, stormy month. Storm after storm marched out of the north piling great drifts along the cliff tops, along the cabin walls reaching to the eaves, and filling the nearby woods with snow so deep that one could not walk in it.

Their small cabin was snug and warm for they kept the fire in the small fireplace burning at all times even throughout the night. Marguerite and Old Damienne took turns getting up during the night to replenish the fire.

The child, Yvonne, grew under the women's care. She was a good baby who slept most of the time, except when she was feeding. As Marguerite nursed the baby, she often listened to the winter winds whistling around the corners of their small home. When she or Old Damienne went out to bring in more wood or to get snow to melt for the water they needed, they felt the piercing cold, and they quickly closed the door to keep the heat in.

Occasionally the skies cleared, and feeble sunlight flooded the land from the sun, which hung low over the southern seascape. Then Marguerite looked over their small plot of land and prayed that the snows would cease and the temperatures would rise, but they didn't.

One morning in late December when the temperature rose to a pleasant degree, Old Damienne remarked to Marguerite, "I'm going to check our wood supply. The way we've been using it, I'm afraid we may not have enough to last the winter."

Marguerite nodded and smiled. "If we need more, there's plenty in the woods."

"That's true, but the snows are deep, and it won't be easy to bring it here."

"Well, we'll wait and see. If we must bring in more wood, then we shall have to do it. While you're at it, check the food supply."

They had stored a large supply of fish, ducks, geese that they had smoked and placed in a cache in the ground. They had dried berries and cherries in birch bark baskets that Old Damienne had fashioned. But the weather was so bad that they had been unable to set traps and snares for the hares and rabbits and other small animals that roamed the snow-filled forests.

Marguerite hoped to augment the foodstuffs they had stored with fresh meat and fish, but she had not done so. She was concerned that their food supply might run low.

Shortly Old Damienne returned. She looked at Marguerite sadly. "We've burned a great deal of wood. If it remains this cold much longer, we won't have enough to last. We'll have to go to the woods and get more."

"How's our supply of food?"

"That's better. We're not using it as fast as the firewood, but we'll have to be careful. If these storms continue, we may run short."

Marguerite smiled. "It would be nice to shoot another bear."

Damienne looked at her in horror. "No, never. Bears are too dangerous. You were lucky last time."

"Yes, you're right. I don't think there are any on the island. I haven't seen one since that one."

Damienne frowned. "I hope there aren't any. It would be another worry to think that such huge brutes were here waiting to make a meal of us."

Marguerite laughed. "You'd make a nice meal."

Damienne did not laugh. "I'm sure he'd eat the child and you before he would try to chew on my old bones. My meat's tough and stringy."

"Enough of such talk. We have things to do. Damienne, I'm going to scout in the woods to see if I can find some trees that I can cut down.

While the weather is pleasant, we must get more wood. We can't run short of wood for the fireplace. Food we can ration, but when its cold we must keep the fires going."

Old Damienne nodded as she bent to toss a small chunk of wood onto the glowing coals in the fireplace.

"Yvonne, should be quiet for a while. She's fed and comfortable."

Marguerite dressed quickly in the woolen clothes that she had brought with her from her uncle's ship. Then she slipped through the door with a heavy blunderbuss in her left hand. Since the incident with the bear, she never went very far from the cabin without the gun. She felt that the gun wouldn't help her if she met one of the demons that Old Damienne insisted inhabited the island, but she knew it would kill any animal that she might see.

She headed away from the cabin pushing her way through the powdery snow that came above her knees. The going was slow, and the depth of the snow increased as she made her way deeper into the woods. Packed animal trails wove in and out among the trees and under the clumps of bushes. She knew that most of them were paths that the rabbits and hares followed as they roamed the woods nibbling on the tender twigs and sweet bark of the poplars and willows.

She stopped and adjusted the burning cord-match in its holder along the stock of her gun. Without that smoldering, glowing fire, her blunderbuss was useless. She checked the priming. Her gun was ready.

As she trudged along, she noted a dry tree here, a fallen one there, that would be available for firewood. She also watched for likely places to set her wire snares and deadfall traps. The still air and the mellow sunlight gave her a feeling of freedom after the confinement of the past days in the small cabin.

Occasionally, a squirrel chattered at her from a tall tree, and once a rabbit scooted away as she almost stepped on it. A number of birds chirped at her as she moved slowly through the deep woods.

Then she spotted a movement ahead of her. It was not that of a small animal such as a hare or fox. She froze and waited. Then she saw it again. A dark spot against the white of the snow. She stared intently into the mass of tree trunks and bushes. It was a large animal, but what was it?

She held her breath, listening. No sound broke the stillness. Slowly she moved toward a large tree off to her left. She lifted her feet slowly, placing them carefully ahead of her, so she wouldn't step on a twig that would snap and break the stillness. Then the spot moved again.

Cautiously she moved from tree to tree so she could get a better view of the animal. Since she was downwind from it, she was sure it had not noticed her presence. Then she saw it: a tall dark animal with a horse's head, but atop the head was a great spread of palmate antlers. The animal tossed its head into the air and turned toward her, sniffing. She had never seen such a large animal on the island before. It stood tall at the shoulders, its massive head moving from side to side as it tried to spot any danger.

Marguerite lifted the heavy blunderbuss and placed it against the tree trunk. As she did so the barrel bumped against the frozen bark with a heavy thump. The animal snorted and jumped back. It whirled about and trotted through the trees waving its head to miss them. Before Marguerite could fire the gun, it disappeared.

When she returned to the cabin, she described the animal to Damienne who insisted it was one of the demons that inhabited the island. Marguerite laughed. "If it was one of the demons, it was more afraid of me than I was of it."

Old Damienne shook her head solemnly. "Marguerite, you must be more careful with those demons. One of these days, one of them will get you. Then what will happen to the baby and me?"

Two days later, Old Damienne burst through the door, her eyes wide with fright. She had gone to get more wood from the pile outside, but she had none in her arms. "Marguerite," she stammered, "there's a white demon outside at our food cache. It's large."

Marguerite carefully placed the baby Yvonne on the bunk, then said, "Calm down, Damienne. What did you see?" She reached for the blunderbuss that leaned in the corner.

"It's white and it's large. It was trying to destroy our food. It wants to kill us."

"You take care of Yvonne. I must see for myself." She did not trust Old Damienne's judgment. More than once the old lady had been wrong, especially when it came to wild animals. She viewed all wild animals as demons that were trying to snatch her immortal soul.

Marguerite checked the priming of her blunderbuss and then lighted from the fireplace the cordlike match used to ignite the powder that fired the ball. Cautiously she opened the door and stood beside it surveying the open area before her. Thirty feet away the large white animal turned toward her. It was a dirty white that blended into the drifted snow behind it. The white turned to a pale yellow as the long fur streamed toward its massive feet. Marguerite recognized it as a bear, the same kind that she had killed months before.

Her heartbeat quickened. This was just what they needed. This animal would replenish their depleted meat supply, and if its flesh was as tasty as the last one, it was a bonus.

The animal turned to face her, its head swinging from side to side, its nose snuffing the air, and its small eyes shifting, trying to locate her.

She raised the blunderbuss to her shoulder, pressing the barrel along the door frame. The animal looked large and fierce. She searched for the small narrow head. When she found it, she touched the match to the firing hole, and the gun exploded.

The heavy ball smashed into the animal's head. It roared, shuddered, and dropped to the ground. A dark red patch appeared in the forehead. The animal was still.

Marguerite couldn't believe her good fortune. It was the second time she had killed a white bear; this one had died easier than the other one.

She called to Damienne, "Look, there's your demon. It's another white bear. It's dead."

The old servant shuffled to the door and gazed at the fallen animal. "Mother of God, she's protected us again."

The next five days, the two women worked hard to prepare the animal. They skinned it carefully, and cut the carcass into manageable pieces. Since the weather was cold, much below freezing each night, they placed most of it in their pit in the ground. Marguerite was pleased that they now had an adequate meat supply.

After they stored the bear, she worked at increasing their wood supply. Each day, when the weather was good enough, she trudged to the woods with her blunderbuss and her ax, and cut trees into lengths that she could manage. Slowly the pile of wood increased. When the storms came, the two women remained indoors, feeding the fire, preparing food, and tidying the small cabin. They were always busy, and time passed quickly.

As the winter lingered on Marguerite noticed that Old Damienne became more crotchety. She grumbled and complained almost incessantly. Each morning as she rose she muttered that her joints ached. She moaned as she moved about the room tending the fire or preparing food. She groaned when she moved from a crouch to a standing position.

One morning Marguerite asked her, "Damienne, are you sick?"

The old lady looked at her disbelieving. "No, my child, I'm just getting old."

Marguerite took a closer look at her old servant. Yes, she had aged. Her hair was whiter. Her face was more wrinkled. Her fingers were more twisted and gnarled. Her shoulders were more rounded and stooped. This wilderness life was not making her younger.

"I do hope that spring comes soon, and then the ships'll come back. One of them will surely find us."

Old Damienne smiled. "I hope so. I'm eager to return to France. Then I can die in peace."

"Damienne, you mustn't talk like that. You're not ready to die yet. But you're right. I hope that the ships will find us."

Winter dragged on; the two women survived. Late in March the snow started to melt as the hours of sunshine increased. Fewer storms came from the north, and sea birds appeared along the coastal cliffs. They enjoyed the return of the good weather, and their spirits enlivened, especially Old Damienne's. As the days lengthened, Marguerite was overjoyed at the change in her old servant; her eyes sparkled, her smiled returned, and her old vigor reappeared. Marguerite rejoiced that they had survived the hard, cold winter.

11. Disaster

Most of the snow had melted. Only small patches remained of the large drifts that formed beside the cabin and along the margin of the woods. Each day more birds returned to the cliffs to mate and nest. The sounds of the noisy birds shattered the wilderness quiet and continued throughout the day and most of the shortened nights.

Marguerite felt that life was renewing for her and her small group. Old Damienne's spirit came alive, and she rejoiced at the return of the birds, the grasses, and the new growth on the trees and bushes. When she found the first pussy willows, she was delighted. She gathered a bouquet of them and presented them to little Yvonne, who was now six months old. The child had grown and developed. She could sit by herself and had to be watched carefully because she was making efforts to crawl about the small floor surface of their tiny home.

Marguerite often gazed on the tiny creature with pride. She was a robust, happy child with dark hair and rosy cheeks. Old Damienne insisted that she was the image of her father, Robert, but Marguerite could see many of the characteristics of the Robervals—active, adventurous, and full of life. She had her father's dark hair and complexion, as well as his dark eyes, but in character she was a Roberval.

One morning in late March, the skies were overcast and a chill wind blew from the sea. Marguerite rose from her bunk, surprised that Old Damienne was not up yet. Usually Old Damienne was the first to rise, because she stoked the banked fire in the fireplace and prepared their morning meal while Marguerite cared for the child.

Marguerite glanced over to the other bunk where Old Damienne slept. The mound of blankets did not move, and no sound came from it.

Marguerite lifted her head and called softly, "Damienne, are you awake."

No answer came.

"The poor dear must be tired. I won't disturb her."

Quietly she rose and dressed. The child also slept. She moved to the fireplace and stirred the mound of ashes gently. A few glowing coals appeared and she added shreds of birchbark to them. A wisp of smoke rose as the resinous material smoldered and then burst into flames. Then she added slivers of dry wood to the tiny flame and soon the fire was rekindled. She crouched before the growing fire, thinking. They had survived the cold winter. Soon the fishing boats would be arriving from France and surely one of them would fish near the island. They would be rescued. She prayed silently, thanking God for his bounty and protection. Her prayers were interrupted by a low moan from Old Damienne's bed. The sound startled Marguerite.

She rose quickly and moved toward the old woman who moaned again.

"Are you all right?"

The mound of blankets and furs moved slightly. Marguerite pulled the covers from the old woman's face. In the dim light Marguerite could see that the lined face was drawn and twisted. She touched the wrinkled forehead. It was cool and dry.

She drew the old woman's face toward her. Her eyes were partly open, the eyelids unmoving. A deep moan escaped from the slack, parted lips. The old woman tried to move, but she was awkward. She tried to speak, but no intelligible sound escaped her lips.

Gently, Marguerite grasped her shoulders and twisted her onto her back. Marguerite felt Old Damienne's muscles tense but she could not move herself. Marguerite realized that the old lady was paralyzed. The eyes stared up at her unmoving, half-open, eyelids unflickering. Marguerite had seen other old people with the same affliction. It came on suddenly, sometimes remaining until death, other times disappearing after a short period. Some recovered completely; others somewhat; still others died.

During the next two days Old Damienne lay quiet and unmoving. Marguerite tried to feed her soups and broths that she made, but the old woman would not or could not swallow the liquids. She couldn't drink the water that Marguerite offered her. She lay silent, breathing slowly and unevenly. Marguerite prayed often that her old servant would recover; how she would miss her if she died.

On the third morning Marguerite notice her eyelids flicker, and her eyes followed Marguerite as she moved. Marguerite patted the withered cheek and smiled at her old friend, "Damienne, you're going to get better."

Marguerite was sure the old woman understood her.

In the following days Damienne improved. She took some of the broth that Marguerite fed her; she drank some of the water that Marguerite offered her. She could move her right hand—the fingers and then the whole hand. The right side of her face twitched and moved, but the left side remained slack and unmoving. She tried to talk, but Marguerite could not understand the gibberish that came forth. When Marguerite wasn't busy with the chores and with Yvonne, she sat beside Damienne's bunk and held her gnarled hands.

Old Damienne's right hand squeezed hers.

Each day Marguerite could see some improvement, some new strength, and more movement. She felt that God was answering her prayers. As the days lengthened and the days became warmer, Marguerite became more confident that Old Damienne would recover.

One morning, Marguerite listened carefully as the sick woman struggled to say something. The first sounds were garbled and unclear, but then she made out the word. Old Damienne was trying to say Marguerite's name. When Marguerite realized what she was saying she clasped the old servant's hands in hers and encouraged her. "Oh, Damienne, that's wonderful. You're improving. In a short time you'll be well again. Keep trying."

A half smile covered the old woman's face, and her grasp increased. Slowly she twisted her head to look toward the gurgling Yvonne on the floor. Her eyes flashed and flickered.

Marguerite moved to get the child and bring her to the bed. The old lady's eyes smiled as Marguerite place the child on the bed beside her.

Some days, Marguerite felt that Old Damienne was improving, but on other days she seemed to drift backward. She lay in the bed unmoving, her breathing shallow, and her faculties asleep. On those days, Marguerite often despaired that her old companion would ever recover. On the days when she seemed improved, Marguerite was sure that one day she would be her servant again. Every morning she knelt beside the old lady's bed and prayed. These moments of prayer seemed to please the sick woman; often her lips moved in unison with Marguerite's although no intelligible sound came forth.

One afternoon as Marguerite returned to the cabin from the woodpile, she heard a loud moan from Old Damienne. She hurried into the cabin and knelt beside the sick bed. Old Damienne had lifted herself onto her good elbow. Her eyes were bright and clear. Her lips worked quickly. She called in a loud, muffled voice, "Marguerite, Yvonne!" Her voice was urgent and demanding.

Marguerite placed the child beside her. Yvonne tried to grasp the old woman's face. The old woman smiled crookedly and leaned forward to kiss the child's cheek. She whispered something, but Marguerite could not understand her. Marguerite leaned over her and grasped her hand. The bony fingers seized hers strongly. A loud screeched escaped the quivering lips; her body shuddered and she fell limply back. Her eyes closed slowly.

* * *

Tears streamed down Marguerite's cheeks as she placed the last spadeful of dirt on the shallow mound parallel to Robert's carefully kept grave. She picked up the child and stood, her head bowed, as she prayed silently for the two people that had shared her abandonment.

The wind blowing from the sea whipped her skirt and hair as she glanced up to the whitecapped waves that rolled into the rocky shore. Robert and Old Damienne could keep perpetual watch for the ships that never came.

She clasped the child tightly to her bosom. Although Robert and Damienne were gone, she could not give up hope. She must struggle on for the sake of the child. The child was her reason to persevere, to continue the struggle, to pray for rescue.

During the next weeks spring turned into summer; the weather became sunny and warm; the birds nested and the young hatched; the woods became alive with leaves and then flowers; insects and other small animals filled the area with life. Marguerite worked on a garden as young Yvonne learned to crawl and had to be watched every minute so that she would not wander away to the cliff's edge or to the woods.

One day in late May, Marguerite noticed that Yvonne fussed and cried more than usual. By now the child had five teeth and when they came out she was cranky, so she thought nothing of it.

The next morning she awoke sensing something was wrong. Her hand sought the child, and she withdrew it quickly. The child felt fiery. Quickly she lifted herself to her elbow and rolled back the covers. She drew the infant to her. As she did so Yvonne screamed. The piercing sound surprised Marguerite. She moved back.

She stared at the child and then crooned softly, "My darling, what's the matter?"

Quickly she uncovered the small body, searching for a rash or pocks, but there were none. The child, although warm and rosy, was clear and unblemished.

"My darling, what's the matter?"

The child wriggled and waved her hands and feet about. Her mouth puckered into a narrow opening and cries came from it as the lips worked.

Marguerite picked her up and drew her against her bosom. The small body felt dry and hot. She touched the smooth forehead; it also was dry and hot.

Fear squeezed at her heart. Her heart pounded against her ribcage. She whispered, "Oh, Yvonne, if only Old Damienne were here, she would be able to help you, child!"

The child cried out as if in pain.

She held the child tightly, rocking her back and forth. But the child's cries became more intense.

"I must bathe you, my darling. That will cool you off." She placed the crying child on the bed and hurried to prepare a basin of water. In moments she bathed the burning body of the sick child. The soothing water had its effect and the child quieted.

For the next two days, Marguerite hovered over the child, bathing her frequently to relieve the fever, rocking her to soothe her, and trying to nurse her, but the child refused to eat. The nights merged into the days; Marguerite napped when she could. As fatigue took over, she couldn't be sure if the child was improving or not. Sometimes she felt that the fever had broken, but at other times she felt that it was worse.

On the third evening, Marguerite could see that the child was worse. Her body burned, her lips were parched, her eyes were half-closed, and her dark hair hung limply about her flushed face. What worried Marguerite most was her breathing which was quick and shallow.

She sat beside the bed staring at the child. She had done everything she could think of, but nothing seemed to help. The only thing she could do now was pray.

The flickering light from the fireplace sent strange moving shadows over the log walls and the child's sunken cheeks. Marguerite leaned over the small form, holding the tiny hands in hers. The breathing pattern changed. It became long and deep and the tiny body shuddered as it tried to obtain air.

Marguerite shook her to wake her, but the child's eyes did not open. The lips did not move. The eyelids did not flicker. Marguerite laid her head on the tiny chest that heaved as it struggled to draw in the life-giving air.

"Dear God," she pleaded, "do not take my child. Please leave me with someone."

The tiny body shuddered and was still.

12. Alone

For two days after she buried her child beside Robert and Old Damienne, Marguerite sat staring out to sea. The high point of land overlooking the narrow rocky beach provided a good view of the ocean to the east. The mid-June weather was warm and pleasant with fresh breezes invigorating the summer air. The days were long and the nights short, so short that there was a continuous glow in the northeastern sky.

Marguerite felt no pain, no hunger, no thirst, just a deep sense of loss. She was now alone and a deep loneliness took over her mind. As she sat staring at the far water horizon, she reviewed all the happy times she had enjoyed with her loved ones. Robert had been kind and loving, treating her as someone special. Whenever he found a beautiful flower in the woods, he brought it to her and presented it as a special gift. Everything he did made her feel that it was especially for her: when he built the small cabin, it was hers; when he captured an animal for food, it was for her; when he increased the woodpile, it was for her. Each time he left to go on some errand, he kissed her tenderly. Old Damienne had been faithful and loyal to the end. Marguerite remembered how she had helped to deceive her uncle when she wanted to meet Robert. Old Damienne understood their love for each other. She encouraged it. When they were exiled to this forbidden island, Old Damienne accompanied them without complaint or argument. She had served Marguerite and Robert, and the child, Yvonne, faithfully. She was like a mother to Marguerite.

The child had brought her such joy. It was part of her. She had watched Yvonne at her breast, and the love she felt overflowed from her, pulsing through her body like the blood that sustained her. She marveled as the child grew and developed; she remembered her first smile; she heard her first gurgling laugh; she saw the child's sparkling eyes brimming with love; she recalled her pride when Yvonne sat alone for the first time, when she crawled for the first time, when she stood for the first time.

Now they were gone, and she was alone. She had nothing to live for. Everyone she loved was buried in the shallow graves beside her. She prayed silently that they were enjoying the bounty of heaven and that God in his love was now looking after them.

She sat on the grassy knoll, staring. She raised her knees and held them in position with her arms. She leaned her head against them. She closed her eyes and listened. The crying birds, the pounding surf, the rustle of the leaves, the swish of the tall grasses, and the buzz of the insects made her realize that the world was still alive. That she was still alive. She must not despair. Although she missed her loved ones, life must go on.

She raised her head and looked about her. Soft fluffy clouds marched to the land from the far sea horizon; the gannets, gulls, and other birds swirled low over the green surf hunting for food; the waves rolled in jagged lines toward the rocky beach, breaking upon the shore in white froth, splashing the cliffs high up; the trees swayed, and the leaves danced. The world was alive, and so was she.

She realized that she hadn't eaten or drunk for three days, and the hunger and thirst struck her with fierceness that she hardly knew existed. She jumped to her feet and hurried to the cabin. She must eat; she must drink; she must continue to live. She must keep watch for a ship that she was sure would one day come.

She would plant a post at the cliff's edge and hang a flag from it so any passing ship might see it. She would keep a signal fire ready to be lit, but she would also keep her cabin, the garden, the woodpile, and her food supply maintained so she could survive even if a ship did not come.

In the weeks that followed, she developed a routine. Each morning she rose and walked to the three graves. There she knelt and prayed for their immortal souls...and her own. Then she prepared her morning meal, which usually consisted of water, salted fish, and fruit—fresh when it was available. Then she cleaned the small cabin although it was seldom very dirty. A single person did not create much dirt.

Following that, she took her blunderbuss and headed to the woods to check the snares and traps that were set there. Sometimes they contained the carcass of a rabbit, a hare, or some other small animal. These she carried back to the cabin where she skinned them, salted them, or cut them into strips and hung them over a smoky fire until they were dry and hard. This and the salt preserved them, and it gave them a different flavor. In the afternoon, she worked in her garden, coaxing the plants to yield vegetables and fruits. When the wild berries ripened, she gathered them— some she dried, and others she ate fresh.

When the weather was fine, she took some clothes that needed mending and, with her needle and thread, she sat on the high point beside the graves and worked as she looked out to sea. But no ship's sails did she see.

Summer gave way to fall. The young birds swirled in large flocks as they tested their newfound wings. The calling and crying built up as the juvenile birds joined their parents in the noisy hunt for fish along the shallow margin of the bay. The leaves turned color; the grasses yellowed; the skies lost their brilliance; and Marguerite knew that it would soon be winter.

Like the animals, she felt the urgency of the season. She gathered and harvested from the woods and her garden. She stored and prepared for the snow and cold that would soon be upon her. As the days shortened the tempo of her activities increased; her woodpile grew; her store of meat increased; her harvest of grains and berries enlarged; and as she saw her supplies grow, she felt satisfied that she could survive another winter.

Each day her resolve to survive increased. She must return to France and tell the world of the injustice and cruelty of her uncle who had condemned her and her loves to the loneliness of this isle of demons.

The winter snows came; the days shortened, and a strange silence fell over the land. But Marguerite kept busy. The fire needed incessant attention; the short hours of daylight gave her little time to do the chores: keeping the supply of wood for the fireplace, preparing her meagre meals, melting snow for water as the small creek behind the cabin froze over, and keeping the cabin tidy. She loved to be busy, but when she found a free moment, she turned to prayer.

The days passed slowly; the winter passed more slowly, but she was comfortable and satisfied. She had an adequate wood supply; there was no shortage of food; her home was warm and cozy; the only thing that marred her happiness was the loneliness. Many times she talked to herself, carrying on an animated conversation.

Occasionally strange sounds pierced the air, coming from the direction of the woods, and her heart beat more quickly, but they never harmed her so she soon forgot about them. She didn't believe they were the demons that Old Damienne said inhabited the island. Most likely they were the call of strange animals, or birds, or some other creatures that she did not know.

One warm, sunny, winter day she decided to take a walk along the rocky beach. The sunshine and fine weather made her feel the confinement of the small cabin.

She dressed warmly and made her way down the path that they had developed to the beach below. The ocean was calm and flat like the surface of a quiet pond. Far out to sea she could see the large, light blue shape of an iceberg. Once, she might have mistaken the triangular shape for a ship, but now she had seen enough to know what it was. She stopped and watched it as it drifted southward to the horizon. She wished it was a ship, a ship that came especially to take her away, to take her back to France, to people.

But it wasn't, so she walked along picking her way slowly through the rocks that were covered with a thin sheen of ice and snow which lay like a white blanket covering the rocks and driftwood farther up the beach.

The ice and snow sparkled in the sunlight, like jewels. Carefully she placed her feet, but not carefully enough. She stepped on a snow-covered rock, and her foot skidded. Before she could catch her balance, her other foot slid also. She felt herself falling, and she flung her arms out to break her fall. Her heavy clothes impeded her movement and held her arms.

She fell forward. She landed with a jarring thud, and the world disintegrated before her eyes. For several moments she lay motionless, in a state of suspended animation. Everything stopped, but she did not lose consciousness. She felt no pain, no sensation at all.

Then the world came alive again. The waves nearby moved. The sun shone. The clouds drifted. She moved her arms; they still moved. She tested her legs; they still moved. Then the pain hit her. She had landed on her stomach. The force had knocked the air from her lungs, stunning her. Now her lungs struggled to draw in the air she needed, but the pain in her chest impeded her lungs from doing so. She tried to push herself up, but her arms had no strength. She rolled to her back. Pain traveled like lightning through her upper body, from her shoulders to her waist.

Slowly air entered her lungs, and she lay gasping. Each intake of air stretched her ribs, and she cried out in pain. She tried to breathe more slowly and less deeply, drawing in air in little gasps. It lessened the agony.

She moved her arms again. There was no pain there. She lifted each leg in turn. There was no pain there either. But each breath sent a spasm through her chest, and she moaned in protest.

The pain lessened, and she tried to rise. But the pain pierced her again, so she lay quiet waiting for it to subside. Her mind cleared, and she assessed the situation. She had injured herself in her shoulders and chest area. Her limbs and lower body seemed unaffected. She hadn't lost consciousness, so she reasoned that her injuries were not fatal. They might be painful, but she felt confident that she would survive.

The longer she lay, the less painful it seemed. She could breathe now with less pain. She moved her right arm. The pain was in her shoulder. It pulled at her muscles, but no bones seemed broken. She tried the other arm. Pain again shot through her shoulder, but again it did not appear that any bones were broken.

Painfully she pushed herself to a sitting position. If she did not move the pain disappeared. Then she twisted to her hands and knees. Pain nauseated her, but it subsided as she rested on her hands and knees. She could move. All her limbs functioned. She could breathe, but the movement was painful.

She struggled to her feet, trying to ignore the pain that wrenched through her. She stood still, waiting for the pulses to subside. They did.

Two weeks later she still felt pain when she moved suddenly or when she turned over in bed during the night. The first day after her accident was lost in periods of pain and misery. She remembered little of the struggle to return to the cabin. The climb from the beach was lost in the paroxysms of pain that weakened her. She recalled the beads of sweat that collected on her brow. She knew that she had rested frequently, but finally she got to her bed.

The next two days were lost as she drifted in and out of sleep. The struggle to rise and restoke the fire—which she knew she must do to keep alive—shattered the fitful sleep that erased the pain. On the third day she awakened her mind clear, and the pain in her shoulders, a dull ache.

She was thirsty; she was hungry. But she knew that she would survive. The pain was dull, and although bothersome, she could rise and move about. She whispered a prayer of thanks. God had punished her, but he had also guarded her. He had protected her. She was alive.

During the next days her life returned to its old routine. The pain subsided and only reappeared when she moved suddenly or differently.

13. Ships

The spring of 1644 came with a rush. By the beginning of May the trees were in full leaf, the grasses along the cliff edges waved in the gentle breezes, the birds sang incessantly, and the sea birds carried on their raucous life along the cliffs.

Marguerite was happy to see winter disappear. She knew that with the coming of spring, the fishermen would make their annual trip to these western shores, and maybe this year a fleet would decide to fish in these waters. Although she had already been on the island for almost two years, she still believed that someone would come by and rescue her, someone from her uncle's colony, some fishing boat searching for better fishing grounds.

As the spring days lengthened, she thought more and more of the possibility of being rescued. She hung one of her old dresses from the pole that Robert had planted; she kept the beacon fire ready to be ignited; she spent many of the daylight hours scanning the sea. On several occasions she saw icebergs of various sizes floating southward, and she saw pods of whales as they frolicked and spouted, but no ships.

One late spring afternoon she sat on the point of the cliff next to the three graves, which she tended carefully, staring out to sea. The gulls, gannets, fulmars, and other sea birds whirled in great flocks from their nesting colonies. Marguerite watched as they hunted for food and quarreled with each other for their catches. From the nests on the cliff sides the young were just emerging, and the parents worked diligently to feed their hungry offspring.

A movement on the far southern horizon caught her eye. She squinted in the sunlight sparkling on the small waves. The reflected sunlight glinted, sending shafts of bright rays into her eyes. She held her right hand above her eyes to shade them. A white cloud bank mingled with the darker blue of the ocean waters, sometimes obscuring the horizon.

She saw it again. A dark strip between the sea and the sky. She rose to her feet straining to keep her eyes on the dim object. She didn't want to lose sight of it. It disappeared. Then it reappeared. She could make out more than one black line.

As she gazed, the small black lines became spots. Her mind cried out. Could they be ships? She tried to control her hopes. She didn't want to be disappointed again. Times before she had seen objects out at sea that she thought might be ships, but they had been icebergs, or whales, or they had disappeared.

As she watched, her heartbeat quickened. The spots were growing. They were approaching her island. Time seemed to stand still as she watched. She stared so intensely that she thought her eyes were playing tricks on her. One moment the spots were on the horizon, the next they were gone. She stared until her eyes hurt. The sun shining on the sparkling ocean made her eyes water. She rubbed them to clear them, and she gazed again toward the spots.

They were getting larger. She could count them now. There were five of them—one large one and four smaller ones. They had to be ships. She was sure she could see the dun color of sails. She squeezed her eyes shut to clear them of the tears that gathered. She kept them shut for several minutes to rest them. Then she looked up again. They were nearer.

There was no doubt now. Five ships were approaching. The large ship in the lead was a two-masted bark, while the others were small ships of various kinds, one a barquentine, another a schooner. She didn't try to identify the others. She must signal them. She must light the beacon.

She took another look to convince herself that her eyes were not deceiving her. No, they were still there, approaching from the south. She felt a cool sweat cover her body. Her mouth was dry and parched. She tingled.

"I must control myself. They're still far out. I must attract their attention."

She stood still for several moments, gathering her wits about her.

"The signal fire," she whispered.

At the apex of the high cliff she had prepared a fire. Fine tinder lay ready to be ignited with her precious flint and steel. Kindling of birch bark and dry strips of fine wood lay neatly ready to be added to the first tiny flames. Larger pieces of dry wood and then pieces of green wood to make a large smoke lay ready.

She hurried toward it, and knelt before the shredded tinder. She fumbled for the flint and steel that she always carried in a pouch at her waist. Her fingers felt wooden and clumsy. She sat back on her heels.

"Marguerite," she spoke to herself, "you must calm down. These are the first ships you've seen since you've been here. Don't make a mistake."

She clasped the steel bar in her right hand and the worn flint in her left. Her fingers were shaking. She dropped her hands into her lap and breathed deeply.

Slowly her quaking muscles quieted, her breathing became regular, and her mind focused on the task she must do.

She straightened up and leaned over the small mound of tinder, shielding it with her body. Then she struck the steel sharply against the flint. A shower of sparks spurted toward the tinder. She struck the flint again. Another shower of sparks heavier than the first struck the fine dry tinder. A tiny wisp of smoke came from the yellow tinder. She set the flint and steel aside, and leaned low over the tinder. She blew gently on the tinder where the wisp of smoke rose. The smoke increased. She continued blowing increasing the strength. The smoke disappeared momentarily, but a glow spread from where the smoke rose. She blew again. A tiny flame burst from the tinder, spreading rapidly.

Quickly she fed the tiny flame shreds of thin birch bark. The resinous material flared into a larger flame. She added more strips of bark and the flame grew. Then she added tiny chips of dry wood that caught and crackled. She smiled to herself. Soon her signal fire would be large enough to attract attention.

The fire grew so she added larger pieces of dry wood. Once these caught, she placed a layer of green, newly cut wood on the flames that sputtered and sizzled. Great clouds of white smoke rose into the air.

She kept feeding the fire, adding dry pieces of wood followed by green chunks and leaves and grass. Smoke billowed forth in increasing quantities. Then she stepped back from the signal fire.

The white smoke rose in the light breeze in a widening column. She was sure it could be seen for a long distance. She was sure the ships would see it and come to her rescue. She looked out to sea. The five ships were still there. But they were no closer than before. She thought they must be at least a league off shore.

She stood for a long time staring at the ships as they maneuvered slowly in the almost calm air. She could tell they were carrying full sail yet they moved slowly along the horizon, northward. They made no attempt to draw nearer to the shore.

She waved her arms and shouted even though she knew that was useless. Finally when her arms became tired, she dropped them to her sides. She dropped to the grass and leaned her head against her knees. Tears of frustration flowed. What could she do to attract the ships?

She would build two fires, one billowing smoke, the other belching flames. Maybe the lookouts would spot one or the other. She wiped the tears from her eyes, rose, and hurried to the fire. She removed a flaming stick and set it ten feet from the smoke fire. Quickly she added small pieces of wood to the flames and the fire increased in size. Like one possessed, she rushed about adding larger pieces of wood to the second fire as she kept the first one going adding more fuel and more green wood, leaves, and grass.

As the flames leaped higher she added more wood. The flames roared and danced and she enlarged the pile of burning branches until the flames rose higher than her head. The heat was intense, so intense that she had to fling the wood onto the glowing bed of coals.

The heat stung her face, and she could feel the sweat droplets sliding down her cheeks from it and her frantic activity. The smoke pinched her eyes and tears mingled with the sweat.

She flung another piece of wood onto the dancing fire and then stepped back. She turned to the sea. The ships had slowed and seemed stopped. Had they spotted her signals? Had they seen her?

She stood staring out over the sparkling waves. She whispered a prayer, "Oh, God, please let them see my signals. Please make them turn to my island. Please, oh God, let them rescue me." She dropped to her knees, clasped her hands, and raised her eyes toward heaven. She had done everything in her power. It was now up to God to help her. The ships seemed stuck on the horizon, unmoving. They did not approach the shore. They had not lowered their sails. Were they becalmed? No, she didn't think so. There was enough wind to keep the vessels moving. They had hove to intentionally, but had they done so because they saw her signal fires.

For the remainder of the afternoon, she alternated between feeding the fires, hauling wood, green branches, and grass, and praying, but the ships did not move. They were too far away for her to see what the crews were doing, but she surmised that they must be fishing although she could not see the small fishing dories that usually spread out from each ship.

The sun crept across the sky slowly. The shadows lengthened. Afternoon turned into dusk. Maybe in the darkness her signal fire would show up more. Maybe someone on one of the ships would see it and investigate.

She gathered more fuel for the fires. She hauled wood from her store. She cut green trees in the woods and dragged the pieces beside the fires. She collected a pile of green leaves and grass. She must be ready to keep her beacons going. She worked frantically throughout the late afternoon and early evening. She was so concerned with keeping the fires going that she forgot to eat.

When she thought she had enough fuel gathered, she threw herself to the ground and sat looking out toward the ships. They hadn't moved. The western sun glinted off the drooping sails making them more visible than before. Yet they ignore her.

She beat the ground with her hands in anger and frustration. They had to see her. They had to rescue her. Tears came to her eyes. She looked at her hands. They were soiled, blackened from charcoal, streaked with green smudges from the leaves and grass. There was a long, bloody scratch along her left wrist. It was dark where the blood had scabbed. As she stared at it, she realized that it smarted, but she didn't remember when it had happened.

The fires were dying. She had to refuel them. Slowly she rose, and wearily she approached them. She couldn't let them die, especially the flaming one. In the approaching darkness, it would be more visible than her smoke signal.

She added more pieces of wood to the glowing embers. Sparks spewed forth, and the wood sputtered as flames licked at the dry bark. Soon the fire was large and growing.

She decided to let the smoke fire die. It would be of little use in the dark.

She turned back to the sea.

The ships had disappeared. They were gone.

14. Ignored

Marguerite slept fitfully that night. She woke many times, and when she was asleep she dreamt, the same dream over and over again. A ship came to her island to rescue her, but just as it approached the shore it would veer off and she could see the demon crew standing by the deck rail, laughing and jeering at her. Then it would disappear and another phantom ship would approach and the same thing would happen.

When daylight came, she felt that she hadn't rested. Her body ached, her eyes burned, her hands felt dry and parched. She felt tired, but she forced herself to rise. If the ships were fishing in the area, they might return.

She dragged herself from her bed, and rushed to the high point. The sun crept over the eastern horizon flinging its rays toward her. She peered out to sea, out to where the ships had been yesterday, but she could only see a mist rising from the waters. It was so calm that the mist rose like a white smoke obscuring the far horizon. If the ships were out there, she could not see them.

The skies were clear. Perhaps in a short while the sun would burn the mist away; she would be able to see, and the ships would come back.

Slowly she returned to the cabin, prepared herself a meal, and waited.

By mid-morning the sun had dissipated the mist and she could see to the far eastern horizon. A light breeze blew from the south rippling the ocean; the sunbeams, bounced off the moving waters, reflected like a myriad of diamonds. It was a perfect day.

She stood, shielding her eyes with her right hand, scanning slowly the far away horizon. Then she saw them. Five dots in the southern distance, moving slowly north, toward her. It must be the same ships she had seen yesterday. Her heart filled with hope. Today they must come; they must see her signals.

Quickly she lighted both fires. One she smothered with leaves and grass, and once again smoke billowed and leaned northward as the breeze carried it. The other, she fed with dry wood, until the flames leaped higher than her head. Then she turned back to watch the ships. Her heart leaped. One of the ships had left the others and was sailing toward her island. She was sure that it had spotted her fires.

It made slow progress in the soft breeze, but as she watched, it grew larger. It was coming toward the island.

She kept feeding the fires. She laughed, she cried, she prayed. Then she sat at the cliff's edge and watched.

Slowly the ship moved. She could see the brown sails filled with the breeze. She could see the dark hull. She could see a flag at the stern; it was still too far away to identify.

But it was headed toward her. It was coming to her island. Her heart thumped with excitement. What would she say when they landed? How would she greet them? It had been so long since she had spoken to another human being.

Then the ship swung about into the wind. What was happening? Why was it turning? She realized the ship was stopping. It had hove-to a half league off shore. She watched as the sails spilled their air and hung limp. She could see the tiny figures moving about on the deck. She could see the tall masts, the drooping sails, the bowsprit jutting out, the high poopdeck and the high forecastle. She cried out, "Don't stop there. Come into shore."

She stood up and waved her arms. The tears streamed down her cheeks. "I'm here. Can't you see me?

But they ignored her.

She looked at her signal fires. They needed refueling. She ran to them, and pitched on more wood, more leaves, more grass. The flames leaped;

the smoke billowed and drifted away in a cloud. She cried, "You must see this. You must know someone is here. You must come to my island."

She clenched her fists; tears streamed down; she waved her arms; she cried out until her voice was hoarse.

But the ship remained just out of her reach—too far away to hear her, probably too far away to see her, but they must see her signal fires.

Exhausted she flung herself to the ground near the edge of the cliff. She watched the ship, as it lay motionless on the sparkling waters. She had done everything she could. She felt helpless and powerless. Her eyes blurred. The sun's rays on the water hurt them. She squinted. She couldn't take her eyes off the ship, which lay just beyond her. It was close enough to see, yet not close enough to make them realize that they must come ashore.

She was sure they had seen her signals, yet they remained far enough offshore that she could not communicate with them.

During the next hour she watched the ship, but it seemed dead. No boats were lowered for fishermen. The ship lay like a whale resting. Then she saw a boat being lowered. Her hopes came alive. Would the boat come ashore? Would they come to investigate her fires? Would they come to rescue her? She tried to still her pounding heart. She talked to herself, calming herself. She watched fascinated as the boat was lowered over the high sides of the barque. She laughed with joy as it hit the water. She watched hypnotically as three men crawled down a rope ladder to the small boat. They were coming for her. They were coming to rescue her. She was sure of it.

The boat moved away from the ship; its oars flashed in the sunlight, rays glinting off the wet blades. She rose to her feet and stood; her heartbeat slowed, her breathing steadied, a great calm came over her. They were coming! They were coming!

She stood serenely watching as the boat approached. The oars stopped flashing. The boat appeared to be stopping. Her confidence was shaken. Had they really seen her signals, or were they looking for a good spot to cast their lines? Would it do any good to cry out, to wave her hands, to jump about? She waited.

The boat stopped a quarter of a league offshore. She could see the three men in the boat. It was a large dory. Two manned the oars, while the third sat in the stern at the tiller. She could even see that they were staring toward her, but they were too far away. She knew they were surveying the island, investigating her signals, but they were being very careful.

She waved her arms and called out. "I'm here. Please come closer. I want to talk to you."

She stopped and studied the motionless boat. The three men appeared to be staring at her, but from that distance she could not be sure.

She beckoned with her arms. "Please come closer. Come into shore. Don't leave me"

The men seemed to understand her. Carefully and slowly they pulled on the oars bringing the boat a few hundred feet closer. Then they rested.

She beckoned again and called out. "Come. Come into shore."

She could see them resting on the oars, facing the shore. The boat rocked gently on the wavelets. But they did not bring the boat closer. She knew they could see her. She knew they were watching her. She beckoned again. She called again. "Please come closer. I want to talk to you." Then the man in the bow waved. She laughed raucously. They knew she was there. She waved her arms energetically. She took off her short coat and waved it over her head. The three men waved back, but they didn't take up the oars. They watched from the safety of the distance.

She waved her coat above her head more vigorously. They must come closer; they must hear her speak.

She watched transfixed as the two men picked up the oars, fitted them in the oarlocks, and started to row. To her dismay they turned the boat and headed back toward the ship. For several moments she stood shocked. Were they leaving? Were they abandoning her?

She screamed, "Come back! Don't leave me! Don't go away!" The sound burst from her lips, exploding from her lungs. She hoped that they would hear that she was a human being.

But slowly the boat drew away from the island; slowly it headed back toward the ship.

She screamed; she waved her arms; she jumped and pranced about. But the boat continued toward the ship. Exhausted, she sank to the turf. She sprawled on the ground her head resting on her arms. Sobs shook her body. Tears streamed down her cheeks. Anger boiled within her as she mumbled to herself. Slowly she calmed and her mind turned to prayer. Exhaustion overtook her; sleep possessed her.

* * *

The creak of oars and the sound of voices awakened her. For several moments she was disoriented and confused. Where was she? What were those noises?

She lifted her head and stared out to sea. On the horizon she could see four ships; to her right was another anchored just offshore, too far away to be the source of the sounds that she heard.

Unsteadily she raised herself to a sitting position. Her signal fires had burned to a glowing bed of coals. She wiped her eyes with the backs of her hands. Her face felt cold and she knew it must be tear-stained. She picked up her short jacket, which she had used as a pillow and shrugged into it.

Wearily she climbed to her feet. Then she remembered the boat that had left her.

She moved closer to the edge of the cliff. She shook her head. A hundred yards offshore was the boat. There were now five men in it. She could see them plainly. The boat had stopped and the men rested on their oars, their heads turned toward the shore, looking up to the top of the point.

Two men held arquebuses along the gunnels of the boat, pointing them toward the shore. The others stared toward her, their faces solemn, even fearful.

For several minutes they stood staring at each other, silent and unmoving. Large hands seemed to squeeze Marguerite's torso cutting off her breath. She tried to shout but no sound came from her open mouth. She tried to lift her arm to wave but it felt leaden and wooden. It would not respond. Her whole body was rigid and would not obey her mind.

The men stared up at her. They also seemed transfixed, paralyzed.

She gasped, and breathed in deeply. She relaxed. Then she shouted, "Good day, sirs. I'm happy that you've come to my island."

Her shout broke the spell, and the men looked at each other. Then they spoke at once. The steersman stood up his hand on the tiller. He shouted, "Who are you? What are you?" One of the men shouted, "It's a demon. It wants to leads us to this island and devour us."

Another shouted, "It looks like a woman. But is it?"

Marguerite stared at the boat in shock. They were Frenchmen. She could understand them. They spoke her language.

She laughed shrilly, unable to control herself. Her laughed echoed over the water surprising the men in the boat and herself.

One man grabbed his oar and dipped it into the water. He cried, "Let's leave this cursed island. That demon will surely entrance us and entice us to that island."

The man at the tiller raised his hand. "Who are you?"

Marguerite breathed deeply. "I'm Marguerite La Rocque de Roberval."

She stopped.

One of the men cried, "She speaks French. She's a Frenchwoman."

Another answered, "Demons can speak any language. That's how they attract their victims. We must leave this cursed island. We must go back to the ship."

The steersman raised his hand again. "Why are you on this island?"

"I was marooned here two years ago by my uncle, Sieur de Roberval."

There was a jumble of voices as the men discussed among themselves the significance of her remark. But they made no attempt to come ashore.

15. Success

The steersman, who seemed to be the leader of the group, shouted, "Are you a Frenchwoman?"

"Yes, I am."

"Where did you live in France?"

They were suspicious. They did not believe her. She answered slowly, evenly. "I lived in Picardy. My name is Marguerite La Rocque de Roberval."

The men conversed among themselves.

"Is your uncle the Sieur de Roberval?"

"Yes. He's the one who left me on this island."

Again there was hurried consultation. Some men nodded their heads affirmatively, others negatively.

The steersman shouted again, "When did your uncle leave you on the island?"

"Come closer and I will tell you the whole story?"

Some nodded in agreement; one or two were opposed. The steersman gave an order, and the oarsmen took up their oars. Slowly they maneuvered the boat within twenty-five feet of the shore. They stopped the boat and waited.

At that distance their voices floated over the waters distinctly. She could hear their mutters and curses. Fear filled their voices. One man in particular muttered against her. "She's a demon. This island is known as the Isle of Demons. Everyone knows that. Every ship avoids this place."

Marguerite shouted, "Don't be afraid. There are no demons on this island. I've lived here for two years. I've never seen a demon."

The man's voice shook with fear. "Demons deceive you and entice you to come to them. She's a demon. She wants to destroy us. We must leave immediately."

The steersman tried to calm him. "Jean, if she was a demon, she could've destroyed us by now. If she's a Frenchwoman, we can't ignore her."

The other men nodded in agreement.

Marguerite called, "I'll come down to the shore to meet you. Please come ashore. I'm not a demon. I won't hurt you."

Again the men discussed the situation. Then the steersman called out. "We'll come ashore, but you must stay there until we land."

Marguerite nodded her head and shouted, "All right."

The two men lowered their arquebuses from the gunnels and took up the oars. Slowly, carefully, they moved the boat toward the shore.

Marguerite remained on the point of the cliff and watched as they approached. Every few strokes, they stopped and stared up at her as if they were expecting her to vanish or to turn into some hideous ogre.

She tried to keep calm. She tried to contain her excitement. These were the first human beings she had seen in over two years. She must be careful not to frighten them away. She knew that they did not believe her story. Some of them still thought she was a demon intent on capturing them. Her heart beat rapidly. Her breathing speeded up. She talked to herself. "Marguerite, be calm. Breathe deeply."

But her heart would not be still. It pounded; it seemed to echo in her ears. The palms of her hands were cold with sweat. She prayed, "Lord, make these men believe me. Don't let them leave me."

The boat stopped fifteen feet off shore. The steersman looked up at her. The others twisted in their places.

"Why were you placed on this island?" The steersman shaded his eyes with his hand.

"My uncle was a tyrant. I was in love with a young man whom he did not accept. I refused to reject him, so my uncle placed us on this island to die."

"Where's the young man?"

Marguerite shook her head sadly. "He died, as did my servant and my child."

One of the men shouted, "See, I'm right. She is cursed. Her lover's died. Her child's died. Her servant's died. She's cursed. This island's cursed. We must get away before we're cursed."

Two nodded in assent. The steersman raised his right hand. "Let's not be hasty. This woman hasn't avoided what's unpleasant. If she was a demon or cursed, she wouldn't tell us this. She must be telling us the truth. How did you survive?"

"There's much food on the island. We built a house of logs, which is just back of me out of your sight. Our necessities were meagre. Food wasn't scarce. Wood's plentiful. There are no demons on this island. If you come ashore, you can see for yourself. You can come up that path to the cliff top and see my home."

"She's inviting us to our death."

The steersman pointed to a break in the cliff where a small stream gurgled through a narrow canyon. "See, beside that stream there's a path leading to the top. The lady speaks the truth. She's no demon, nor a witch. She speaks the truth."

"I won't go up that cliff. Have her come down. We'll talk to her from here." All the men nodded in agreement.

"Madame de Roberval, please come down to the shore so we may see you better."

"I'll come."

She turned to the steep path that led to the rocky beach. Slowly she made her way down. The men in the boat watched her carefully, suspiciously.

Once on the beach, she found an appropriate rock and sat on it. "See, I'm flesh and blood. I'm not an apparition…or a witch…or a demon.... I'm Marguerite de la Rocque de Roberval of Picardy, niece of Jean Francois de la Rocque, Sieur de Roberval, viceroy of King Francis and lieutenant general of New France. I was with him on his expedition to found a colony in this new land."

"I don't believe her!"

There were several moments of silence as the occupants of the boat peered at the strangely attired young women. She wore a short velvet jacket, which was tattered and torn, over a full skirt that came to her ankles. It, too, was bedraggled: the hem was ripped and uneven. She wore a pair of crude leather shoes that she had fashioned from bearskin. Her face was smoke-blackened and streaked from the tears she had shed. Her hair was long and straggly.

"Please come ashore," she pleaded.

One of the men, a dark-haired, heavy-set man, picked up his arquebus, leaned against the gunnel, and pointed it at her. Another, his companion on the foreseat, picked up his arquebus and held it pointed at the steersman. He spoke in a low, ominous voice. "She looks like a demon."

The steersman peered at the open muzzle of the weapon pointed at his chest. "Look, Jean, if you'd been abandoned on this island for two years, I'm sure you'd look like a demon too. She's suffered enough. We must land and help her." He reached for the tiller.

The heavy gun wavered slightly. "I don't believe her. She's a demon. She wants us to come ashore, and then she'll capture us and devour us. Turn the boat around."

The steersman, a short, wiry man continued, "We're five. She's one small woman. She can't overpower all of us. There's nothing to fear."

Marguerite rose from the rock upon which she sat and moved slowly to the water's edge.

The man whose arquebus was pointed at her spoke in a shrill, quavering voice. "Don't come closer. I'll shoot!" The fear in his voice stopped Marguerite.

The man with the other gun said evenly. "We won't go ashore. Men, pick up your oars and let's head back to the ship."

The two other men grabbed their oars and started rowing. The heavy boat moved.

"Please, please, don't leave me. I've been here for two winters…alone for the last one. You can't leave me."

"Men, we can't leave her. We must believe her."

"We can and we will. It's her life or ours. She'll destroy us. I've heard of this island. Many fishermen know of it. They say it's haunted. Anyone who lands on it is never seen again. They're enticed by a woman demon."

The steersman laughed. "I've heard that story too, but no one's proved it's true. You're cowards."

"Grab that tiller, my friend." The voice was ominous, threatening. "If you don't, we'll let you join that woman demon. You can be her victim. But I won't be."

"Jean, that's a good idea. Let me go ashore. I'll prove to you that that woman isn't a demon…or a witch. I believe she's what she says she is."

"No! If we get that close, she'll capture us. No! We must go back to the ship."

The boat moved out from the shore. Now the second man swung his arquebus toward the steersman who shook his head in disbelief.

The second man grunted, "Jean's right. We can't take a chance. That woman's too dangerous."

As the boat drifted out, Marguerite stood silently staring at it. What must she do to convince these superstitious men that she wasn't a demon? They wouldn't believe her.

"Look, men." She took her rosary from her pocket and waved it before her. "Would a demon have a rosary of Our Lady? Please believe me. I'm not a devil. I'm not a demon. I'm a poor Frenchwoman who's been away from France for a long time. Please don't leave me."

"Another trick. Another trick to get us ashore."

"Jean, demons, devils don't use the Lord's things to accomplish their desires. That woman's telling the true. Let's return to shore. Let me go ashore. I'll prove her story, and then you can come ashore. I'll climb the path and see her house and the other things she must have."

Jean lowered the weapon slowly, but the other man gripped his more firmly. "Why should we endanger our lives? If she's lived on that island for the past two years, she can continue to do so. She's not our problem."

Marguerite raised the rosary before her. "For the Mother of God, don't leave me, don't abandon me." Her voice shook with emotion. She held back her tears with a great effort.

All the men turned toward her. She looked forlorn and sad. A bedraggled apparition on a rocky shore. She begged again, "I pray God, have mercy. Please take me from this island. I'm alone. I'm tired of striving. I need help."

The oarsmen stopped rowing. One turned to the other. "We must help her. She sounds sincere. Her story makes sense. I heard of the expedition to the west to found a colony. I was at St. John's two years ago when Commodore Cartier arrived with his five ships. They were going farther west to set up a colony."

The other added, "I was there when Roberval's fleet was there. I remember some rumours of a niece who was a problem because she was in love with one of the members of the expedition. Maybe she is telling the truth."

"You see, men, her story seems to be true. I believe her. We can't leave her. We must check it out. I'll go ashore…alone, if I must…but we can't leave her alone."

The arquebuses lowered. They picked up their oars.

16. Farewell

Marguerite watched the men take the bundles she had prepared and hoist them to their shoulders. They started down the path to the narrow, rocky beach.

She called to the wiry steersman, "Michel, I want to spend a few minutes up there." She pointed toward the high point of land where he could see three crude wooden crosses. He nodded in understanding.

Marguerite left the group and moved slowly up the narrow path that led to the high point. Since the fishermen had decided to believe her story, time had moved quickly. Although it was early afternoon, they wanted to get back to their ship as soon as possible. They urged her to collect her few personal things and to abandon most of the objects that had become part of her life for the past two years—the crude furniture, the furs, the clothes, and the other utensils that she had fashioned, but as she picked and chose, she found it difficult to discard these treasured objects. Each one reminded her of an incident in her long stay, or it reminded her of the loved ones she would be leaving behind. Robert's clothing—his jerkins, his boots—reminded her of him, of his sensitivity, of his thoughtfulness, even of his weakness.

The meagre objects that were Old Damienne's personal effects reminded her of the love and loyalty of her old servant. And the tiny clothes that she had fashioned for her child filled her with longing and a sense of loss.

She moved slowly up the path toward the three rocky mounds that were their graves. She stood staring at the crosses that she had planted at the head of each grave. Who would tend the graves when she left? There would be no one; the weather and time would remove any evidence of their existence. The crosses would rot and disintegrate. The mounds would slowly level out and grasses and bushes would grow over them. Soon their existence would disappear.

The past years had been happy ones. She had known love; she had known loyalty; she had known motherhood. Robert had been tender and kind, considerate and loving. She knelt beside his grave and prayed, "Dear God, love Robert as I have loved him. He was a good man. He loved you and he loved me." Tears misted her eyes. She bowed her head, oblivious to her surroundings. Her heart filled with love. She moved to her servant's grave. "Damienne, you were like a mother to me. I know you loved me…and I loved you. I know you're in God's heaven. You're still looking after me. I can't take you with me, but I wish I could."

She turned to the smallest of the three graves. She bowed her head. She remembered the tiny body that had been part of her. She recalled its warmth and softness, and her heart filled with love and affection. She could still see the tiny blue eyes, the button nose, the heart-shaped lips, and the pink cheeks. Tears flowed in rivulets down her cheek. She whispered, "Oh, God, why did you take my precious baby? I loved her so much."

"Hurry, Madame, we must leave." The voice called from the beach at the base of the cliff.

Marguerite bowed over the small mound. "My darling, I must leave you, but I know God will look after you." She wiped her eyes with the back of her hand. She rose slowly. She stood for a few moments unable to move.

An impatient voice called, "Madame, we must go!"

She turned slowly and trudged down the path toward the small cabin that had been her home for over two years. It was crude and small. The stone and clay fireplace was rough and crooked, but it had warmed the small room, and it had cooked her simple meals. The logs of the walls were shedding their bark as a snake sheds its skin, but they had protected her from the elements. The birch bark covering the roof needed repairs, but it had repelled the rain and the snow. It was her home.

She stopped and looked into the room. Memories came flooding back: the happy times with Robert, the quiet talks with Old Damienne, the precious moments with Yvonne, and the times of sorrow.

She turned away quickly and hurried down the narrow path along the tiny stream that flowed to the bay. Each step down brought a tear to her eye. She felt that she was abandoning life. She felt that she was leaving her heart behind on the high cliff at the graves, in the tiny room of the crude cabin, in the woods behind, and on the beach below.

The five men were gathered around the heavy wooden dory, looking toward her. She could see the impatience in their eyes. They had stowed her few parcels. They stood like sentinels on each side of the boat, hands on the gunnels, ready to shove off.

Michel, the steersman, called, "Hurry, Marguerite, we must go."

She came up before them. "I can't leave."

Five mouths dropped open.

"I can't leave. My loved ones are here. I must stay with them."

Silence hung like a heavy pall over the group. The five men stood staring at her. They shuffled their feet. Then Michel spoke. "Madame, you can't stay here. Your loved ones are dead. They don't need you any more. They're in God's hands now."

The others nodded in assent.

Marguerite looked at the ground. She brushed her right hand against her eyes. She gulped. "That may be true, but I can't leave them. Who'll tend the graves? Who'll remember them? Who'll…?"

"Madame, they don't need your care. Their souls aren't in those graves. They're in heaven. They'll be with you wherever you go. You can do nothing for them here."

Again the men nodded. One groped for words. "Madame Roberval, you must come with us."

She lifted her eyes. These were the same men who earlier that day wanted to leave her. These were the same men whom she had pleaded with to save her. "I can't go with you. I must stay here. My life's here. The people I love are here. I need them. I must stay."

She stepped back.

17. The Return

The four men turned toward Michel, the steersman. The taller one took a step forward. "Michel, we can't stay here forever. Soon it'll be dark and we won't be able to find our way back to the ship." His voice was crisp with annoyance.

Another added, "Michel, we've done all we can for this women. She's being unreasonable. I say, if she wants to stay here by herself with her memories, let her. Let's go." He stepped back toward the boat.

Michel looked at the rest of the crew. They stood silent; their faces, masks.

"Madame, I think you're being foolish. You've survived for two years, but at what cost. Your three companions are dead. If you'd been in France, they might still be alive."

Marguerite stood unmoving, her hands clasped. Could not these men understand? Her loved ones were here; they were not in France. There was no life for her back in France.

Michel continued, "You must make a new life for yourself with your family in France. You can't stay here. It's not right."

Her mind heard what he said, but she didn't answer. She thought of France. The only family she had in France was her uncle. The rest of her family was dead. And the uncle she had once loved had rejected her. It was he who had placed her on the island. Probably by now he had assumed ownership of her lands since he was her next of kin.

"I've no family in France. My uncle was my next of kin, but I'm sure he's had me declared dead."

"Madame, you judge your uncle too harshly. I'm sure he'll be overjoyed to see you."

Marguerite laughed, high-pitched and derisive. Her uncle was a cruel, harsh man. She had heard many stories of his anger and of his savage punishments. As an army commander, he expected absolute obedience to his commands. Anyone who disobeyed was cruelly punished, and he had continued that behavior as commander of the expedition. How she had been fooled by him. How she had misunderstood him. No, he wouldn't be overjoyed to see her. He probably would deny that she existed.

"No, I'm sure that my uncle won't be pleased to see me."

"Madame, you can't stay here. It's not right for a young woman to live here alone without anyone. Please come with us."

One of the oarsmen murmured, "Madame, we can't wait much longer. You must come with us."

They were probably right, but her heart told her that she was right. She belonged here, with Robert, Damienne, and Yvonne, not in France where she had no one, where life would be a struggle to obtain her place in French society. She would probably have to fight to get her possessions back. She would probably have to struggle with her uncle in the courts and she knew that he had many friends among the nobility. He was a personal friend of the king. She would never be happy in France while here she would work to provide herself with the necessities of life, and that was easy. The island provided all the things she needed, food, shelter, even clothing. Why should she go to France?

"I'll stay here."

The four oarsmen started pushing the longboat from the rocky shore.

Michel stared at her. "Are you sure you're making the right decision, Madame."

One of the men grumbled, "Let her be. If she doesn't want to come with us, there's nothing more we can do. We must leave."

Michel peered at the bedraggled figure before him. She looked forlorn and sad, almost pitiful. If they left her, she would surely perish. If not this year, then in the future. She would die alone and unattended. It might be several years before another fishing fleet would approach these shores. He could not leave her. "Madame, you must come with us. If you do not come, I'll feel guilty the rest of my life. I'll feel that I've condemned you to a lonely death."

She raised her eyes to his. She could see his sincerity in them. These men were trying to help her, to be kind to her, to rescue her, and she was making it difficult for them.

"You must come back to France and tell everyone of your experience, of your uncle's cruelty, of your struggle, of the struggle of your loved ones. You must come to France and fight for them. You must let everyone know about them." He was right. She mustn't let her uncle get away with the injustice he'd done to her, to Robert, to Old Damienne, and her child.

"Michel, if she doesn't want to come, leave her."

Another suggested, "Let's take her. Once she's aboard ship she'll change her mind."

Michel raised his hand to stop them. "Madame, we must leave. I implore you. Come with us. You'll not be sorry." She nodded her head. The men smiled as they helped her into the boat.

Epilogue

Marguerite de La Roque de Roberval returned to France, but little is known of her life upon her return. There is some evidence that she made her home in the seaport town of La Rochelle where she spent the rest of her life as a teacher. There is no evidence that she married or had any more children.

Two people told her story, Andre Thevet, a historian at King Francis' court and King Francis' sister, who was quite a court gossip. Both stories are the same except for some minor details.

Printed in the United States
19719LVS00007B/190